Because of Thomas

Because of Thomas

Sara Tatham

Bob Jones University Press, Greenville, South Carolina 29614

Library of Congress Cataloging-in-Publication Data

Tatham, Sara, 1950-
Because of Thomas / Sara Tatham.
p. cm.
Summary: When she returns from Mountainside Christian Academy to her family farm in New Hampshire for the summer, fifteen-year-old Liz faces a struggle between her family's faith and her own desire to "be herself," a struggle complicated by her older brother's battle with muscular dystrophy.
ISBN 0-89084-794-0
[1. Christian life—Fiction. 2. Brothers and sisters—Fiction. 3. Muscular dystrophy—Fiction. 4. Physically handicapped—Fiction.] I. Title.
PZ7.T211415Be 1995
[Fic]—dc20 94-39817
CIP
AC

Because of Thomas

Edited by Debbie L. Parker
Cover by John Roberts

Greenville, South Carolina 29614

Printed in the United States of America

ISBN 0-89084-794-0

15 14 13 12 11 10 9 8 7 6 5 4 3 2 1

In memory of Tim,
whose life touched so many people.

Chapter One

"I'm sorry, Mom and Dad, but I won't be going back.

"I wasn't really happy there.

"I won't go back! You can't make me!"

All during the long bus ride from Mountainside Christian Academy to my home in northern New Hampshire, I'd been rehearsing the words I meant to say the moment I arrived. The bus had passed through rural farmlands, and grimy industrial towns, and quaint villages, and still I was no closer to the way I wanted to present my case than I'd been when I left school. I kept picturing the hurt in my parents' faces—and, even worse, the puzzled frown and worried blue eyes of my brother, Thomas.

I couldn't get them out of my mind: Dad . . . that hard-working, red-faced farmer—honest, upright, and about the gentlest, most loving man I'd ever known. Mom . . . slim, pretty and young-looking, though she carries a workload almost equal to Dad's. Soft-voiced, until she loses her temper, but she doesn't do that much anymore. And then Thomas . . . dark-haired, blue-eyed Thomas, sitting patiently (and sometimes not so patiently) in his wheelchair; shoulders slumped, legs immobile, and arms nearly so, but nonetheless keeping the household on an even keel. My older sister, Mary Rose, came into focus less clearly. She's married and lives only a few miles from our farm, but it's not like she's still at home. Besides, she has a little boy, Noah. Even though she and her husband, Roger, are partners in Fox Hill Farm with Mom and Dad, Mary Rose has her own life to live.

And I wanted to start living mine! I really did love my family. It's just that I wanted to be *myself*—Liz Williamson—not some mindless jelly poured into a mold they'd picked out for me.

As far back as I can remember, our family has been different. In the beginning, it was because we lived on a farm and all the other kindergarten kids lived in town. Then, when I was about seven, I learned that we were different in another way. Thomas, my big brother, had muscular dystrophy. He would be spending the rest of his life in a wheelchair. As I grew older, Mom and Dad told me more about the disease and explained to me that he'd probably live only until he was about twenty-one.

So, naturally, our family's life centered on Thomas. I can't remember a time when our activities weren't bound by his limitations. Mary Rose had told me about family vacations—trips to Maine and Cape Cod. But I couldn't remember them. Restaurants, for us, were usually limited to take-out places. If they had steps at the front door, they were no good for Thomas. Of course he could be carried up stairs, and Dad had often done it, but Thomas's sense of balance was so affected by the disease that stairs terrified him.

It was a big burden for any family to carry, but I always felt my parents were equal to the task. Still, it shouldn't have come as a surprise to me when they started to think about God.

They'd never had much time for church, but now they dug out the family Bible and began to read it. Scripture verses and phrases like "born again" started to drift around our house.

One evening at supper, Mom said, "I heard a minister on the radio today. You know," she explained, "one of those spiritual thoughts they put on in the middle of the day, right after the news and weather."

When Dad looked at her expectantly, she went on. "Tom, the things he was saying . . . well, they sounded just like what we've been looking for. Do you think we should call him? I wrote his name down."

Dad served himself some more mashed potatoes before answering. "It couldn't hurt, honey; I'd be glad to talk with anyone who might be able to help us."

Chapter Two

And that was how we came to know Pastor Ronald Nelson. He arrived the very next afternoon. After Dad invited him in, he had prayer with us and began to talk about crops, livestock, and the farm he'd grown up on. Dad asked him something about the Bible, and he told us that he believed the whole Bible, without reservation.

"Why, so do we," said Mom. "We've been praying that we'd find someone who could explain it to us—how to be right with God and live His way."

"Well, it's very simple," said Pastor Nelson. He told us how man's sin had separated him from a holy God, and how God had sent His own Son to earth to bridge that gap.

I hadn't known that. I'd heard the Christmas story, of course, about how Jesus was born in a manger. But I never really thought about *why* He came.

The pastor explained how Jesus had died on the cross for us; that He'd paid the penalty for our sins. Anyone who wanted to could pray and ask forgiveness of God because of what Jesus had done. Then he said, "Years ago I asked Jesus to be my Saviour and take control of my life. He's been a wonderful Friend ever since. Would any of you like to make that decision right now?"

I felt uncomfortable and squirmy inside. This wasn't something I was ready to do. But Mom and Dad said that they would. Then Roger and Mary Rose both said they wanted to be saved too.

I looked at Thomas. He was pretty thoughtful. I didn't think he'd fall for this without thinking it over more. But to my surprise, he nodded his head in agreement.

"Sometimes," he said, "people think that because I'm in a wheelchair, I never do anything wrong. Why, once at a family reunion, I even overheard Great-Aunt Ida say that I'd surely go to heaven, because I'm so good." He shook his head. "That's just not true. I've done plenty of wrong things, and I've had some bad thoughts too. I need forgiveness just like anyone else."

Pastor Nelson prayed with each of them individually. I was thankful he hadn't turned to me and said, "Well, Liz?" like I figured he'd do. But when he was leaving, he shook my hand and said, "You've been pretty quiet this afternoon, Liz. How do you feel about the things you've heard?"

I shrugged. "I'm going to have to give them a lot of thought."

And that was where matters had stood for the past few years. I went to church with the family every time the doors opened. And at least once a week, the invitation to be saved was repeated.

"Not today," I'd tell myself. "It's fine for Mom and Dad. They need help. Roger and Mary Rose . . . well, naturally, they want to please Mom and Dad. Thomas? Well, he doesn't have much else to do with his time. And he probably worries about dying. But not me! I've got a lot of living to do before I tie myself down. Besides, everyone here is praying for me right now. I will *not* give them the satisfaction of seeing me respond to that invitation."

Meanwhile, I was living a double life. At school I was part of the most daring crowd. But I was careful to keep my grades up. I *did* like learning new things, even if it wasn't quite the "in" thing to do. Besides, all my teachers still remembered Mary Rose's brilliant work and the dogged determination that had helped Thomas to graduate from high school. I knew I couldn't let my grades slip.

But eventually I stopped worrying about that too. Exams were coming up, and my friends thought it would be fun to simply not show up during exam week. That, we thought, would really be making a statement about just how much school meant to us. Each day of that week found us killing time in a different park or fast-food place. By the end of the week we were pretty bored, and, also by the end of the week, my homeroom teacher got suspicious. She called our parents, and the game was over. We were all suspended until after Christmas vacation.

Mom and Dad were terribly disappointed in me. They even talked to Pastor Nelson, and to my disgust the whole church prayed about it at prayer meeting. I knew Thomas and the rest of the family were praying about it at home too.

One night during the holidays, Mom knocked on my door while I was reading in bed. "Liz," she began softly, "you've been offered a wonderful opportunity! How would you like to start all over at a new school in southern New Hampshire, a Christian school? Pastor Nelson can arrange it all, honey, if you're willing to try. Because of the good grades you got before all this happened, the school is willing to take you."

So that's how I happened to go to Mountainside Christian Academy. I hated it from the first day. Oh, not all of it, of course. The school was tucked into a corner of a quaint old New England town. The school buildings were charming houses with antiques all over the place. And many of the teachers were better than those I'd had in public school. They really made me think.

But the kids! Actually, I guess there wasn't much wrong with them, either. But a lot of them seemed to talk about the Bible and God all the time, and they wore dressy clothes to class—a lot different from my usual sweatshirts and jeans. And we had to go to chapel every single day. The thing that bothered me most was the feeling I had that everyone knew my whole life story; they were probably praying for me too. It was disgusting!

Chapter Three

Now it was June, and I was traveling home again. Mom and Dad would simply have to understand that I wouldn't be going back to school. Maybe I could point out to them how expensive it was—a waste of money they couldn't afford.

I turned my attention to the window again. Just a few more stops and I'd be home with the family. I knew there'd be a welcome at the Foxville bus stop; a supper of all my favorite foods; and an evening walk around the neighborhood. I had to admit I was looking forward to it.

Before long the bus slowed to a halt. Here was Foxville, its little corner of courthouse lawn and two park benches dignified by the title of Bus Stop. I jumped off the bus and waited impatiently for my luggage, looking around for the family. My father's pickup truck was parked up the street in front of the post office. I was surprised and a little worried. I expected the whole family to come in the van and meet me. They always drove the van because that's the easiest way for Thomas to travel.

I looked again. Dad had hopped out of the truck and was heading toward me, whistling cheerfully. I relaxed a bit. Nothing was seriously wrong then.

I ran to meet him. "Dad! Hi!" was all I managed to get out before he enveloped me in a bone-crunching hug. "Where are the others?" I croaked.

He scooped up my bags and started back to the truck. "Thomas is pretty tired," he said over his shoulder, "and I guess your mother's putting the finishing touches on a fancy supper."

"Has Thomas been sick? I can't imagine him feeling too tired to come meet me. Why didn't you write?" I got into the truck while Dad tossed my luggage into the back and then climbed in beside me.

"Liz," he began as we chugged out of town, "uh, Thomas does get tired quite easily now. You know the nature of his disease, honey. It gets . . . uh. . . ."

"Progressively worse," I said in a flat voice. "I know. But that doesn't make it any easier." I hated even thinking about the subject, much less talking about it.

"It's hard on Mom and me too," Dad said quietly. "We've had to watch Thomas weakening day by day. That's why I've been hoping that maybe you could relieve your mother of some of Thomas's care this summer. And you know it always lifts his spirits to have you home."

I began to perk up. I could make this a good summer for Thomas and start to repay my folks a little bit of the love they'd spent on me. But I didn't like the somber note in Dad's voice.

"Are you trying to say this might be Thomas's last summer?" I asked bluntly.

Dad winced. "It's hard to say. At twenty-two, Thomas has already outlived the average muscular dystrophy victim. But he's not afraid of death, Liz, and you mustn't fear it for him either." He looked me right in the eye. "Now let's talk about something more cheerful. Thomas will want to see you smiling, and it'll do Mom good too."

"Are—are the wild strawberries ripe yet?" I asked. Just the thought of picking the tiny red jewels and spending time in the grassy meadow was enough to make me smile.

"Your brother has made me check every day. I think there are plenty of ripe berries, with enough green ones coming along so you can pick every day for a while, if you like."

"I'll go tomorrow," I said. "That is, if Mom doesn't need my help. Could I take Thomas along?"

"A short outing shouldn't tire him too much. You could take him when you pick in the upper pasture, since that's accessible from the road."

"You don't have to explain that to me!" I laughed softly. "Don't you realize I know every square inch of this farm?"

Dad smiled. "I know you do, Liz. Guess I'm becoming forgetful in my old age. Sure do get tired quicker than I used to."

Then we turned in at the driveway to the farm. I've always been glad that the first Thomas Williamson built his house at the end of a long, tree-bordered lane. The house itself is of white clapboards with black trim. There are window boxes overflowing with red geraniums. And there's a ramp, with railings, leading to the front door; Mom has bordered it with brilliant yellow marigolds.

"It's as beautiful as always," I told Dad. "Don't ever change a thing."

He chuckled. "Think you might be just a little bit prejudiced?" He parked the truck, and we hurried into the house.

Mom met us at the door. "Liz!" Her voice was as warm as her hug. "I declare you must have grown another couple of inches! Are your clothes still long enough?"

"Well, they are for the moment, but . . ." I hesitated. This was not the time to blurt out that if I had my way, I wouldn't be needing anything new for school except some jeans.

Mom didn't even notice my hesitation. She turned excitedly to Mary Rose, who was setting the table in the dining room. "Did you hear that, honey? You'll have to crank up your sewing machine. Liz will need a whole new wardrobe this fall!"

I waved at my sister across the room. It was hard to imagine I'd ever forgotten what she looked like. She's just a shorter, slightly plumper version of me, except that her dark hair is short and mine is long. But I was looking around for someone else. "Where's Thomas?"

"In his room, Liz, lying down. He's just taking a little rest before supper. Go on down and say hello. I don't think he's asleep."

"Who *could* sleep, with all the racket you're making out there?" Thomas called from his room down the hall. "Liz, get in here and let *me* see how much you've grown."

That was Thomas, always the big brother. I dashed down the hall and into his room. I'd planned on giving him a big hug, but he looked so thin and frail I was almost afraid to. Instead, I bent down and gently kissed his forehead.

"Thomas, old boy, how's it going?"

He grinned. "Can't complain. And how about yourself, Lizard? You're looking great!"

His use of the old childhood nickname brought quick tears to my eyes, but I blinked them away. "I *ought* to look good. In fact, it's surprising I haven't gained fifty pounds. You should see the way they feed us at school."

"Cinnamon rolls?" He named my lifelong weakness.

"Homemade," I assured him. "With nuts and raisins. In fact, I even managed to talk the cook into sharing her recipe. I don't think I could survive the summer without them. I'd probably go into withdrawal."

He laughed out loud at that, then sobered. "Mom has so much on her hands now, Liz. She doesn't bake as much as she used to."

"No problem," I said airily. "The recipe is super simple, and I intend to bake the rolls myself. Weekly."

"I can't wait to try them. Liz, how do you really like school? Have you had a pretty good semester, all in all?"

"Well, pretty good. Um . . . some of the classes have been really interesting. It's just—"

"Liz? Could you come fill the water glasses? Just as soon as Dad gets Thomas up, we're going to eat."

"Coming, Mom!" I patted Thomas's shoulder and hurried to the kitchen. Thank goodness Mom had called me before I'd been forced to answer his question. Thomas always saw too much.

Supper was a festive meal, for which Mary Rose, Roger, and Noah joined us. As usual, Mom had worked too hard, but it tasted wonderful—and Mary Rose had helped with the preparations when she wasn't busy keeping Noah out of trouble. There was baked ham with pineapple sauce, one of Mom's specialties. And baked potatoes, buttered peas, and tossed salad. Her bran muffins too, with real butter. And for dessert—

"Strawberry shortcake!" I said. "Mom, you didn't . . ."

"No, dear, I wouldn't even think of encroaching on your wild berries. These are from the Evans's farm stand."

Everyone was still laughing over that as Mom, Mary Rose, and I cleared the table. Then Mary Rose started the dishes, and Mom hurried around putting away leftovers. I stood around with a dish towel in my hand, watching red-haired Roger playing with Noah on the living room rug. Dad had taken Thomas to the bathroom.

It was all so familiar! And it was so good to be home, but I still felt uneasy, thinking about how I was deceiving them all. Sooner or later, the school issue would have to come up. Part of me wanted to get it over with, but the cowardly side of me wanted to put off that discussion indefinitely. Mom and Dad were obviously working hard right now, and I could see that they weren't getting enough rest. Maybe I could relieve their load a bit. And then drop the bomb? It was a dilemma all right, and I felt guilty just thinking about it.

Chapter Four

As it turned out, I needn't have worried about anyone guessing my thoughts. Roger and Mary Rose left early, and Dad fell asleep in his recliner even before that. It made me feel terrible to see him nod off like that—more like an old, old man than a healthy farmer in his early fifties. I knew Dad had always been exceptionally strong, physically. It was scary to realize he wasn't as invincible as I'd thought.

Thomas cleared his throat noisily. When I glanced his way, he frowned a little and said, "He doesn't get very much sleep at night, Liz. I—I haven't been sleeping too well. I just can't seem to get comfortable; my back aches a lot. So . . ."

He didn't continue, but I knew what he was trying to say. Muscular dystrophy victims, especially those as far advanced in the disease as Thomas, can't turn themselves over in bed as ordinary people can. That means someone must turn them during the night. In our house, that job usually falls to Dad, because Mom is such a heavy sleeper. I was later to learn that for Thomas, a "good" night was one in which he woke Dad only three or four times.

I looked around the quiet living room. "Uh . . . do you ever go for walks in the evenings anymore?"

Thomas straightened up a little. "Sure, sometimes," he said. "I'm just kind of tired tonight, so I don't really feel like it. It's pretty humid for walking, anyway."

It seemed to me that he was protesting a bit too much. Mom glanced up from the magazine she was flipping through. "It's cooling off some now, Thomas," she said. "If you'd like to take a walk, Liz, you go right ahead. Don't worry about the rest of us. Maybe we've gotten too set in our ways around here. We'll perk up, now that you're home."

An idea struck me. "Maybe I *will* go for a short walk, just to the upper field and back. I'll scout out the best berries for tomorrow. Want to go strawberry picking tomorrow, Thomas?"

He shrugged. "Why not? But I'd think you could wait till tomorrow to see the place too." He sounded almost jealous.

"Now, Thomas," Mom said. "Liz is a big girl. She knows what she wants to do. She's had a long bus ride, and she's eaten a big meal. No wonder she feels like a little exercise."

That was all the encouragement I needed. I opened the door to the hall closet and took out my hooded sweatshirt.

"Thanks, Mom. I won't be long."

I slipped out of the house through the screen door, down the farm lane, and out to the tar road. Maybe the cool evening breeze would clear my head. The air was fragrant with the delicate scent of wild roses, and from the woods a white-throated sparrow trilled its last song of the day. As I trudged along, my thoughts were anything but peaceful. Thomas, my parents, and the kids at school chased each other through my head, moving faster and faster as I climbed the hill.

And there at last, just across the road, was my favorite berry patch. But I wasn't ready to search out strawberries yet. I sank down on the gray stone wall beside the road. A chipmunk watched me warily, then scampered off toward a butternut tree.

I tried to arrange my thoughts into some sort of order. Even from this distance, I could still look back at school with a feeling of alienation. I couldn't go back there. I just knew they were all praying for me. Probably praying that I'd get straightened out and be like them. As if I wanted to be like them! All I wanted was to be myself.

Now if I could just get my parents and Thomas to see that. Thomas was a reasonable, thinking person. He could see both sides of an issue; he was always doing that about political things and then writing letters to the editor or one of our congressmen. So if I could talk to Thomas first, get him to see my view, then maybe he'd help me talk to Mom and Dad. After all, they weren't *un*reasonable. Mary Rose is her own person, and so is Thomas. It's just that the lives they've chosen echo the values of Mom and Dad's. My parents couldn't see that I needed to be different, to be free to choose my own way. But—and this was another worry—what *was* my way? Who was I, really?

I took stock: Elizabeth Leigh Williamson, fifteen and three-quarters years old; medium height, rather thin; black hair, blue eyes; skin that tanned so deeply that, at summer's height, I resembled my half-Indian great-great grandmother. Perhaps it was from her, and from the long line of Williamsons who'd farmed here, that I took my deep-rooted love of this land and all that grew on it. I shrugged. It was growing dusky under the trees; time to look the strawberries over if I intended to.

I got up and stretched, feeling cramped from my perch on the rough stone wall, then crossed the road and let myself through the gate. The long grass was damp as it swished about my ankles, and the spicy scent of pine hung over everything. I bent and quickly parted the grass at my feet, searching for the plump red berries hidden beneath. Yes, there they were, hanging round and ripe from long slender stems. I picked a cluster, stem and all, to take home to Mom. She'd often told us kids about the berry-picking expeditions of her childhood, and she still showed a child's delight in an especially nice bunch of berries.

I straightened up and began to move closer to the woods in search of another good spot. Branches crackled nearby—birds, probably. It never ceased to amaze me that such tiny creatures could make so much noise. I took another step, and the crashing in the woods grew louder. I knew it couldn't be birds, chipmunks, or squirrels. No, whatever it was must be a pretty good size, and I didn't think it was a dog. I whistled, just to make sure. Bruno, the farm dog, might have followed me, though he usually stayed pretty close to the barn. The noises increased. It probably *was* Bruno then, responding to my whistle.

I clapped my hands. "Bruno! Here, boy! Come on!" I whistled again, shrilly. The crashing sounds came closer, but no tail-wagging, tongue-lolling Bruno emerged from the woods. And in the deepening dusk, I could just glimpse a shadowy form through the trees. A bear!

Did one run from bears? Did one stand still? This was no time for debate. I turned and ran, flinging myself over the bars of the gate and pelting down the hill as fast as I could go. As I ran, I thought hysterically of my Great-Grandmother Williamson, who'd been stalked by a bobcat as she pushed her baby's carriage along this very road. "She knew it was there," went the family legend, "but she just kept right on walking." Well, so much for my sentimental notion of being a throwback to my ancestors. I was a disgrace to them! My sweatshirt hood flopped against my back, and my running footsteps made loud slapping sounds on the tar. My chest was hurting, and I could feel a pain beginning in my side. As soon as I arrived at the lane that led to the farm, I stopped to catch my breath.

Light spilled from the farmhouse windows—from the bathroom, where Thomas would be brushing his teeth; from the living room, where Dad drowsed in his chair; from upstairs, where Mom would be turning down my bed. It all looked so ordinary and calm that my fear evaporated. If it hadn't been for the pain in my chest, I'd have thought I dreamed the bear, or whatever it was. I took another deep breath and turned down the lane, toward the house.

I managed to get to my room without a lot of talk about my frightening experience, and I surprised myself by falling asleep as soon as I tumbled into bed. I slept soundly until the sunlight poured into my room.

Chapter Five

I always think my room looks its best in bright sunshine. This morning, since I'd been away so long, it looked extra good, with its pine-paneled walls and wide old floorboards. I smoothed the bedspreads on the twin beds, admiring them once more. They're the color of oatmeal, with a woven-in design of green pine trees, trimmed with red. I had even painted my bookcase to match: dark green with barn-red shelves.

I dressed quickly and hurried downstairs, lured by the scent of frying bacon. Mom turned from where she stood at the stove, flipping pancakes. "Good morning, Liz! It looks like a really nice one, doesn't it?"

"Sure does!" I said. "I've got my day all planned."

"You slept late enough, didn't you?" said Thomas, as he sailed into the dining room with Dad, so to speak, at the helm. Dad pushed him close to the table, set the wheelchair's brakes, wedged a back wheel securely with a triangular block of wood, and settled Thomas's elbows on the table edge.

"That's enough out of you," I told Thomas. "Seems to me you usually eat breakfast earlier than this, yourself."

"Ah, but I waited for you, dear Lizard. I'm dying to hear your story of last night's spine-tingling adventure in the berry patch. Dad, of course, has given me his version."

Mom hurried to the table with a plateful of steaming pancakes. "Ask the blessing, Tom, so we can start right in while these are hot. And Thomas, don't you tease Liz about last night. She's not used to being in the woods after dark, and any little noise—"

I opened my mouth, but Dad looked quickly around the table and said, "Let's pray."

After the prayer, I went on with what I'd intended to say. "Those were not *little* noises! Whatever was making them was the size of a bear, at the very least. And I'm not at all sure I *didn't* see a bear!"

The effect on my family was disappointing. Dad said, "Hon, please pass the syrup."

Mom said, "Have some bacon, Liz, and here's the butter."

So Mom didn't believe me either! If she thought there was even the slightest chance that a bear was in those woods, she'd never allow me to take Thomas anywhere near them. Instead of telling me what I should eat, she'd be fussing around and asking Dad if he *really* thought. . . .

Oh, well. I'd better just enjoy breakfast. Whatever was there, it wouldn't be likely to bother us in broad daylight. That decision reached, I stacked three pancakes on my plate with lots of butter and syrup, added some home-cured bacon and poured myself a glass of orange juice.

"Do you eat like that at school?" Thomas demanded.

"No, I don't take this much of anything. It's good, but it's not Mom's cooking, and it isn't homegrown. Besides, I expect to be busy enough this summer to work off every calorie."

"Liz is right, Thomas, so no more remarks from you about what she eats," scolded Mom.

I knew the main reason Thomas noticed what I took was that he was very careful of what he ate. He knew it was an effort for Dad and Mom to move his helpless body around, so he ate only enough to maintain his weight and stay healthy.

I pushed back my chair, stood up, and carried my plate and silverware to the sink. "Want help with these dishes, Mom, or anything else before Thomas and I take off?"

"No, dear, I don't think so. It won't take me five minutes to wash up these few things, and then I'll plan on spending the rest of the morning in the office."

Mom kept the farm books, and I knew she appreciated the times when the house was empty and she could work uninterrupted.

"Get ready then, Thomas," I said, reaching into a cupboard to get some plastic containers for our berries.

Ten minutes later we were on our way. It was hot and humid, and I puffed with the effort of pushing Thomas up the steep hill. I paused for just a moment, gazing at the beautiful New Hampshire countryside. The air seemed to be filled with the scent of ripening wild strawberries. Our destination lay just ahead, a high, sloping field that was surrounded on three sides by woods. Even though part of the field had been turned into a sand pit, the remaining tall grass still hid hundreds of strawberry plants. I always thought it worked out well that haying time came just after strawberry season. Sometimes they overlapped, like this year, but my considerate father and brother-in-law would hay this field last, giving me plenty of time to pick.

Suddenly, for no reason that I could name, I felt uneasy. It was ridiculous, in this quiet place filled with sunlight. But I shivered.

"I don't know, Thomas," I said. "Maybe I'll go on and try the slab yard instead."

The slab yard is a big field near the sawmill where they used to pile the bark-covered sides of logs that are removed before they saw logs into boards. The field is empty now, and it's covered with straggling little strawberry plants.

"Oh, come on," said Thomas. "The berries aren't as good there, and you know it. They're a lot smaller too."

He was right. The slab yard was definitely the second-best place to pick strawberries. Still, a feeling of uneasiness gnawed at me.

"Come on," Thomas said again. "There can't be any danger here in the daytime. Not within sight of houses and everything. Besides, Mom and Dad didn't seem to think there was anything to worry about."

"Oh, all right," I agreed. But I couldn't shake off that nagging feeling, even as I opened the gate and maneuvered the wheelchair along the edge of the sand pit. I kept thinking about those funny noises, and wondering—

Suddenly the wheels of the wheelchair sank into the deep, soft sand. The chair tipped over, and Thomas flew out, face first. I was so appalled by what I'd done that I couldn't think what to do next.

"Turn me over!" Thomas gasped. "Turn me over! I've got sand in my mouth!" He was spitting out grains of it with each word.

"Okay!"

Carefully I helped him to a sitting position, propping him in a most precarious way against the fallen chair. Mom's horrified face flashed into my mind as I sat cross-legged in the sand beside him to unscrew the cap of the thermos bottle we'd brought along. I poured icy water into the cup and helped Thomas to gulp it while I tried to decide what to do.

"How are we going to get you back in?" I asked him.

Although I'd helped Dad lift Thomas many times, I'd never done it alone, and I wasn't sure I could. He outweighed me by ten or fifteen pounds—all of it dead weight.

But Thomas didn't answer me. His face was pasty white as he pointed to something written in the sand, only a few feet from us. Large, wobbly letters spelled out the words: I WILL NOT HURT YOU.

"Looks like your bear knows how to write," Thomas said with a nervous laugh.

"Don't try to be funny!" I snapped. "I'd rather it *was* a bear! How do we know what kind of lunatic wrote this?"

I knew my voice was shaking, but I couldn't help it. All kinds of crazy explanations rushed through my mind. I shivered, and turned despairingly to Thomas. "How are we going to get out of here?"

Chapter Six

"Can I help?" asked a voice above me.

I jumped. A pair of blue denim knees were just inches from my face. They belonged to a tall, broad-shouldered young man about my own age. He had a hammer sticking out of his pocket and a grin on his face.

I looked at him suspiciously. "Are you responsible for *that*?" I asked, gesturing toward the wobbly writing.

He looked rather sheepish as he admitted, "Well, uh, yeah, I guess I am. I knew I'd scared you away last night, see, and I had to find some way to let you know it would be okay to come back, that you hadn't heard a wild animal of some kind." Brown eyes glinted behind his glasses. "But look, hadn't we better get your brother back into his chair?"

"I don't even *know* you," I began, but he was already lifting Thomas and settling him in the wheelchair, gently brushing sand off his dungarees.

"I'm Steve Todd," he said. "I'm fixing up that old hunting camp in the woods."

"This land is posted against trespassers," I said firmly. It belongs to my . . ." My voice trailed off as I noticed the smile on Thomas's face, and the barely concealed amusement in the stranger's eyes. Then I remembered something Thomas had said earlier. Suddenly I was plenty angry.

"Wait just a minute," I said. "How does this person know I'm your brother, Thomas Rowe Williamson III?"

They both began to laugh hysterically, which made me even angrier until I realized what I'd said. Then I couldn't help grinning to think how funny I must have sounded, and I went on more quietly.

"All right, how does he know we're related, then? Obviously, you two have met before."

"Let's start again," the boy said quickly. He held out a large, brown, capable-looking hand. "I'm Stephen Todd. I'm spending the summer working for Mr. Evans down the road, helping with chores, haying, and assorted carpentry jobs. Your dad's letting me use the hunting camp in exchange for fixing it up a little. You must be Liz. I've heard lots about you from Thomas, and I'm glad to finally meet you."

It was impossible to stay mad at him. He had such a steady, serious look, but I'd seen a gleam of humor in his eyes.

"I'm glad to meet you too," I said as politely as I could. "But I really wish someone had told me you were here. I wouldn't have spooked so easily last night, *or* this morning."

"I didn't get a chance, Liz," Thomas said. "Everything was so rushed yesterday, and I never even connected Steve with last night's 'bear'."

"I can explain that," said Steve. "It turned cooler than I'd expected, and I had to scrounge around for some firewood. I felt awful knowing I'd scared you off, but I thought running after you, or yelling, would only make matters worse."

"You're right, of course," I said gloomily. "I'll be only too happy to forget last night and pretend we just met."

He smiled widely. "That's settled, then. But I'm afraid we'll have to get acquainted some other time. I'm due down at the Evans's to help with the haying."

"Steve, come for supper tonight," Thomas said. "We're having strawberry cream pie!"

"Sounds great! I'll be there!" Steve waved, then disappeared into the woods. In a minute, he appeared on the road, jogging steadily toward the Evans farm.

I turned to Thomas in a mixture of anger and relief. "How dare you promise him strawberry cream pie when we haven't even picked *one* berry yet?"

Thomas smiled at me. "I have faith."

"What you have is insanity, if you think I can pick the quart of berries that recipe requires, *and* get home and make pastry, *and* whip the cream . . . in fact, the way that guy probably eats, we'll need *two* pies. Well, if I'm going to pick two quarts of strawberries, I'd better get at it."

I sank back into the tall grass and began picking rapidly. I wanted to bring up the subject of school, but I knew I'd lose momentum if I took my mind off my work. So I picked steadily for a long while, and Thomas entertained me by bringing me up to date on all the family news.

During a break in the conversation, I heard his stomach growl, and I jumped to my feet. "Thomas, what an idiot I am! You must be starving—it's after one!"

"I guess I am getting a little empty," he admitted.

"Well, look, we must have nearly two quarts here," I said quickly. "If the pies are a little short on berries, it's a sure thing Steve Todd will never notice."

"What have you got against him, anyway?" Thomas asked as I piloted his chair carefully out of the sand pit. I'd tucked the containers of strawberries snugly in beside him so that I could give all my attention to driving.

"Who?" I asked, when we were safely out on the road again.

"Steve, of course. I hoped you'd like him as much as I do, but you seem pretty antagonistic toward him, Liz."

"I hardly know him, remember? We just met a few hours ago, for about five minutes."

"I know," Thomas said doggedly, "but I've known him for less than a week, and I feel as if I've known him my whole life. He's just that kind of person."

I was silent. He was that kind of person, I had to admit. But that didn't change anything.

"What's he doing around here, anyway?" I asked, just for something to say.

"He told you, Liz! Helping at the Evans's. Lending Dad and Roger a hand too, when they need it. You know Dick Evans isn't getting any younger, and with his son and family gone away to Bible school, he really needs help. When Pastor Nelson heard about it, he recommended Steve. He needed a summer job, and he's a hard worker."

"What do you know, we're home!" I wheeled Thomas inside, ready to end the conversation.

Minutes later, feeling cooler and cleaner, Thomas and I were wolfing down ham sandwiches and iced tea.

Mom came into the dining room and sank down into a chair. "Liz, dear," she said, "I know it's the first day of your vacation, and you probably have plans for the afternoon, but—"

"Mom, as I said before, I want to help out any way I can this summer."

"It's just that I've got a deposit that really should get to the bank today. If you wouldn't mind staying here with Thomas, I could take it in. Dad and Roger can't leave the hayfield, and Mary Rose is trying to catch up on laundry."

"Go right ahead, Mom," I said. "Thomas, here, has rashly promised his friend Steve Todd strawberry cream pie for supper. So he can hull berries while I make the pastry."

Mom looked doubtful. "I hadn't planned anything much for supper," she said. "Thomas, aren't you a little too tired for company tonight?"

"Steve isn't company," he said. "The hamburgers and potato chips you had planned will be plenty good enough, and Liz's pies will make it a feast. As for my being tired, I'll lie down the minute we're finished with the berries."

"Well, if you're sure, maybe I'll do my grocery shopping while I'm in town." She headed for the office.

After Mom left for town, I set Thomas up at the table with a colander for the hulled berries. He couldn't work very fast, but his fingers were still nimble. Then I assembled the ingredients for pie crust and began that job.

When my pie shells were baked, I sat down to help Thomas with the hulling. With two of us working, it didn't take long. I put some of the berries into a saucepan with sugar and cornstarch to make the strawberry glaze. Then, while that was chilling, I whipped cream and began assembling the pies. It was only then that I remembered Thomas's nap.

"You're supposed to be lying down!"

He grinned. "That's right; I am. Well, finish your pies. Then you can flag down Dad or Roger on their way to the barn and ask them to help."

The pies were safely stowed in the refrigerator when I heard Dad's heavily loaded truck groaning its way out of the field. I hurried to the door and waved my arms at him.

Dad got out and said, "Whew! I'm ready for a break anyway. Liz, while I'm getting Thomas settled, you might fix a jug of iced tea for us."

After Dad left, I washed up the dishes and was trying to find something in Mom's spotless house that needed doing, when Thomas called, "Liz, come down and talk to me."

I went down the hall and into the cool, darkened room.

"Can't sleep?" I asked softly.

"No, I wasn't really sleepy anyway—just tired, if you know what I mean. And I haven't had much chance yet to ask you how you really liked it at Mountainside."

This was it: the moment I'd been both dreading and hoping for. I pulled the brown leather hassock closer to Thomas's bed and sat down.

Chapter Seven

"Well," I began, "it wasn't bad. Like I said last night, the food was great. All homemade and plenty of it. And I really enjoyed the atmosphere," I went on, warming to my subject.

Thomas leaned forward slightly, his eyes bright with interest.

"I mean," I went on quickly, "the old New England bit. That part of New Hampshire was settled and civilized while this area up here was still just woods. The houses are so interesting and historical, and they're crammed with antiques."

"What about the classes?" Thomas asked.

"Most of them were pretty good." I said. "American Literature was my favorite. Mrs. Ross really made it come alive. She's a writer too, a published one, but she loves all the early American writers. And math—well, you know I've never liked it, but geometry wasn't too bad. I got it out of the way, at least. I won't have to take any math next year."

"I've heard they have a good history teacher there," Thomas said.

"Mr. Donovan. He *is* good. He teaches geography too. He makes it really interesting, and he gets the best out of the kids. It's like he knows exactly what each one of us is capable of and makes us live up to it."

"I liked biology too," I went on. "The science department is excellent. And there are some good elective courses too, like art and photography. I learned a lot," I concluded. "It's a good school. But of course we won't know the whole story till my report card comes."

Thomas sighed in satisfaction. "You know, Liz," he said, "I'm so thankful you can go to a Christian school. I've regretted so many times that I wasn't saved when I was your age. Of course," he added, "a boarding school wouldn't have worked out for me, anyway."

He tipped his head back onto the pillow and closed his eyes for a minute. Maybe I wouldn't have to bring up leaving school just yet.

I should have known better. Thomas was simply rallying himself for another onslaught.

Now he pounced. "What about the other kids? You haven't said a word about them. Did you make any special friends? And how about the spiritual side of things? Chapel? They must have some fantastic speakers."

If I took it very, very, slowly, and answered each question carefully, I might be able to make him see. "Well," I began, "I guess the reason I haven't said much about the other kids is that none of them made much of an impression on me. They all sort of looked the same, all neat and well dressed, and all the girls have the same sort of hairstyles—" I laughed. "Not much like mine," I added, fingering a strand of my long, straight black hair.

Thomas laughed too. "Your hair looks terrific just the way it is," he said. "You wouldn't seem like Liz if you wore it any other way. But go on."

"Well, they—they were nice enough, I guess. They were polite and helpful. But nobody was really very friendly. Maybe it's because I came in the middle of the year. Mr. Miles, the guidance counselor, said that's always hard. And some of those kids have been at Mountainside ever since seventh grade, so they all know each other. But nobody really asked me to spend time with them, or do anything with them, or—"

"Then shame on them!" Thomas interrupted. "But what about your roommate? Wasn't she even friendly?"

"Oh, sure, she tried. It wasn't easy for her, being pried away from roommates she really liked, to room with me and Make Things Easy for me. She studied a lot; she likes to keep up an *A* average. Well, I do too. And when she wasn't studying, she was upstairs in her old room, visiting. But I can't really blame Jane. She did try, at first, to include me in things. Then, when it became obvious that I wasn't fitting in, she just . . . well, stopped trying so hard."

Thomas was looking at me suspiciously. "Just what does that mean: it became obvious that you weren't fitting in? Does it mean what I think it means, that you didn't even try to fit in? Because if it does . . ."

"Thomas," I said, slowly and patiently, "I *don't* fit in, you know. I don't belong there. I said it was a good school, and it is. But it turns out perfect little Christians. I'm not one, and I never intend to be!"

I'm afraid that last remark sounded a little more final than I meant it to. Thomas stared at me. "Liz," he began, then stopped to clear his throat. He took a deep breath to start again, but he began to cough instead. He coughed for what seemed like five minutes, but it was probably less than one. "I'm . . . all right. This happens sometimes. It's like . . . like there's dust in my throat. It tickles and then . . . then. . . ." He was off again.

I stared at him. Mom had left me in charge, and here I was, just standing here, letting him cough like that. He tired too easily anyway, and it could be tiring to cough, as I well knew from the time I'd had a bad cold last winter. Surely there was something I could do!

"Thomas?" I asked during the next lull. "Is there something I can do to help? Get you a drink, or—"

He nodded vigorously, not daring to speak. I hurried off to the kitchen. I didn't think just plain water would be very soothing to an irritated throat, and I had used up all the iced tea mix on Dad and Roger. I supposed Mom would be bringing some when she came. The orange juice was all gone too. Ginger ale! I sped to Mom's emergency shelf. She always keeps at least one bottle of ginger ale on hand for times of sickness. But we were out of ginger ale too. I cast about for something, anything. From Thomas's room I could hear the beginnings of another cough. Then I remembered—milk shakes! Thomas had always loved them, and Mom often fixed him one as a between-meal snack because they were so nourishing. The cold smoothness ought to be especially soothing sliding down his throat.

I hardly dared to look in the freezer, but, yes, there was a little bit of vanilla ice cream left in the corner of a carton. I hurriedly scraped it into the blender along with milk and chocolate syrup. While it whirled, I got out a tall glass and hunted for a straw.

When it was ready, I hurried into Thomas's room and presented it with a flourish. His eyes lit up with appreciation, and he leaned forward so I could help him sip it.

"That's good," he breathed when he had drained half the glass. "Guess I just needed something to wet my whistle. Here's Mom," he added as his quick ears caught the sound of the van returning. "Help me get the rest of this down, and then you can give her a hand with the groceries."

I stifled a smile as I returned the glass to the kitchen. Still the same old Thomas! He seemed to have stopped coughing. But I noticed, as I went to open the door for Mom, that he was still clearing his throat rather noisily.

Mom struggled in under the weight of two full bags of groceries. "Liz, I'm terribly sorry. I didn't mean to take so long," she said, thrusting one of the bags at me. "I just kept running into people I knew, and most of them wanted to talk. Is Thomas still napping?"

Fortunately, she didn't wait to hear my answer, but went out after another load of groceries. I followed her out, and she handed me two more bags. "He's still sleeping, then?" she asked.

I shifted the bags enough so I could open the door for her. "Well, actually," I said as we went in, "he's just been resting, Mom. He said he didn't feel sleepy, only tired. He . . . well, he wanted me to sit and talk with him, so I did. He just had a sort of coughing spell, though."

"Oh!" Mom quickly set down the bags she was carrying. "Go through these bags, will you, dear, and put the perishable things away. I bought some chicken, so get that into the refrigerator first. I'll go check on Thomas."

She vanished down the hall, and I began putting groceries away. I had my head in the refrigerator trying to make room for the chicken when she returned. "He's resting now," she said. "He still has some thickness in his throat, and I'm sure all that coughing wore him out. I've told him we'll plan supper for six instead of five-thirty, to give him more time. The men can use that extra half-hour to clean up, anyway."

When the groceries were all taken care of, I worked on fixing carrot and celery sticks for supper. I stuck them in ice water, then filled a small glass dish with some of Mom's mustard pickles, and a large bowl with potato chips.

"Here's more iced tea mix," Mom said. "Or do you think lemonade would be better?"

We decided on lemonade, and I was putting ice cubes into a big pitcher when Thomas began coughing again, and Mom rushed off. At that moment, Dad came in.

"Problems?" he asked, removing his sweaty, dusty hat and cocking a sunburned ear in the direction of Thomas's room.

"Coughing spell." I tried to match his tone. "The second one this afternoon, and Mom seems worried."

Dad raised his eyebrows. "Hmmm. Well, I'm going to clean up and shave. If he's still at it when I'm done, it might not be a bad idea to get hold of Dr. King and see what he thinks."

He disappeared into the bathroom. I set the table slowly. I didn't really think that Thomas's near argument with me could have triggered that attack of coughing, but I supposed it was possible. Was he still coughing? The noise of the shower drowned out everything else. I took special care with the table, using the blue woven mats and the delicate blue and white china. There wasn't much else I could do until I knew how Thomas was.

At that moment the shower ceased. Yes, he was still at it. Perhaps not quite so steadily, but still at it. Dad stuck his head out the bathroom door, his face covered with white shaving cream.

"Rosalie? Think maybe we ought to let Dr. King know about this little problem?"

Mom stepped into the hall to speak to him. I knew she'd probably been waiting impatiently to ask *him* that very question. But you would never have known it from her voice. "Whatever you say, Tom. I'm sure it's nothing to worry about, but we should probably keep him informed."

Dad nodded. "I'll call him as soon as I've finished here."

Just then Thomas started coughing again, and Mom popped back into his room, but she did it with no impression of haste. They weren't going to let Thomas see their concern.

After Dad had talked to the doctor, he came out into the kitchen where I was trying to decide what to do next. "You haven't started anything for supper that can't wait, have you?" he asked.

I shook my head. "No. Why?"

"Well, Dr. King thinks he should take a look at Thomas. In our situation, you can't be too careful. So he's going to meet us at the emergency room in fifteen minutes. It shouldn't take very long, and we'll plan to eat the minute we get back, okay?"

Chapter Eight

The whole incident had been more than a little disturbing, reminding me that Thomas was becoming, as they said, "progressively worse." I slumped against the kitchen counter and watched them leave. I don't know how long I leaned there, thinking of what Dad had tried to tell me gently on the ride home from town yesterday—that Thomas might not see another summer. I stared blindly out the window at Mom's beds of old-fashioned flowers. Why, they'd been there every summer of my life—it was impossible that Thomas should never see them again.

"It isn't fair!" I shouted, and I pounded the counter top angrily.

"What isn't?" asked an amused male voice. I hadn't heard the screen door open, but there was Steve Todd, grinning widely.

"Don't you believe in knocking?" I demanded.

He was looking around him as he replied absently. "Sure I do, but your folks have made me so welcome here that they've actually told me not to knock."

"Oh, really?" I asked.

"Yes, really! Your dad said that sometimes they're busy with Thomas and might not hear me at the door, so I should just come on in. Where is everybody, anyway? Is Thomas just getting up?"

"No," I said. "They've taken him to the doctor." And I told him what had happened.

"That's too bad," Steve said quietly. "But Liz, Thomas is in good hands. He wouldn't want you to be worrying like this."

"Doctors make mistakes!" I cried. "And *nobody* can stop that horrible disease from progressing!"

"Not yet, they can't," he agreed. "Maybe someday they will, maybe even in our lifetime. But I didn't mean Thomas's doctor when I said he was in good hands. I meant he's in God's hands. There's no safer or better place to be than that."

Not you too! I almost groaned. From things Thomas had said, I had gathered that Steve was a Christian, but he seemed so different from the kids at Mountainside. I couldn't believe he really thought the way they did, but here he was proving it. As I turned away from him, I heard my family coming in the back door. At least I wouldn't have to say anything right now.

I dashed to the stove and turned on the gas under the frying pan, then added the hamburger patties I'd made and refrigerated earlier. I put the buns in the oven to warm and went into the living room to see what was going on.

Dad was wheeling Thomas to his room.

"He's going to lie down again," Mom said. "This whole business has tired him out."

Steve was edging toward the door. "In that case, Mrs. Williamson, I'd better come back another night. Those pies will keep, won't they, Liz?"

I nodded, but Mom was replying, "Now, Steve, we talked about that on the way home. Thomas wants you to stay and eat with us anyway. He might feel like getting up a little later, or at least he'll feel like visiting with you, so please stay. We'd love to have you."

"That's right," Thomas echoed from his room, but I thought unhappily that he sounded like a weak imitation of his usual self.

In spite of the circumstances, supper was a success. We were all so hungry that it tasted really good. Steve and Dad had two helpings of pie each, and they praised it generously.

"Liz is our pastry cook," Dad said, grinning.

Steve refused Mom's offer of a third slice. "I'd love another, but there's just no room." He patted his stomach emphatically.

"I'll wrap up some for you to take home," Mom promised, rising to clear the table.

I stood up too, and began helping her clear the dessert plates.

"Oh, no, Liz," Mom protested. "This is your vacation, dear, and you've worked hard all day. Why don't you and Steve get out for a little walk while it's still light?"

"What about Thomas?" Steve asked. "Won't he be disappointed if he gets up and I'm not here?"

"It was his idea," Dad put in. "He said he hadn't thought about Liz missing our evening walks until she came home and mentioned it. He'll feel more like visiting when you come back."

As Steve and I started down the lane, I muttered, "Don't feel like you have to do this. Honestly, I love my brother, but he always thinks he knows what's best for people. In fact," I added candidly, "that's something I don't understand about this business of being a Christian. I thought people were supposed to *change*!"

Steve smiled down at me. It was a nice smile, I reflected, not his usual irritating grin. "Are you going to make me do some serious thinking on top of a meal like that?" he asked. "I might be able to explain it, but my mind's been boggled by all that strawberry pie! That's one thing I sure am enjoying about being up here—the food!"

"Better than you're used to?" I asked jokingly.

"Way better. My mom never did a lot of cooking; just mixes, and frozen and canned things. Since she and Dad divorced, it's been more of the same, only he and I eat out a lot. But I was thinking that, if you and your mom gave me some of your recipes, I might be able to learn to cook."

"Sure you could," I replied. "If you can read, you can cook."

We were approaching my favorite stone wall and without either of us saying a word, we both moved toward it and perched on the weather-beaten rocks.

"This is a beautiful spot," Steve said. "What a view! The mountains all around, and the green fields spread out down below us. . . ."

"The scent of new-mown hay . . ." I teased.

"Even that! It smells great, even if it does mean a lot of hard work for somebody. And I'm glad to have this job. The money I'm earning means I can do something I've wanted to do for a long time."

"Really? What's that?"

"Go to Granite State Christian College this fall."

I don't know what I'd been expecting, but it wasn't this. "You're kidding!" I said.

"Why should I be? What's so strange about that?"

"Oh, I don't know," I hedged. "I thought you already went to a Christian school, I guess."

"Nope. Dad says he pays taxes to support the public schools, so that's where I've gone."

There was another question I just had to ask. "Did you know that Granite State is right near Mountainside Christian Academy, where I . . . went to school this past year?"

"Only a few miles away," he agreed. "Wish I had parents like yours. Dad wants me to go to the state university. He won't pay a penny toward Granite State."

Suddenly I was curious about him. My parents had pushed me into a Christian school; his were against the idea.

"What's your family like?" I asked.

He laughed. "Well, Dad is tall and thin—no, I know what you mean, Liz. Let's see. We live in Bayport; always have. For a city, it's not a bad place to live. It's pretty nice, really, being spread out around Grand Lake the way it is. Our house is right on the water, close to Dad's work. He owns Lakeview Lumber. You've probably seen the signs."

At my nod he went on. "We have a big old house with gray shingles and dark red trim. Dad and I live there alone now, because he and Mom divorced when I was eleven. She works for a cosmetic company and travels a lot, so they both thought I'd be better off with Dad. And I have been."

"Won't your father miss you this summer?" I asked.

Steve shook his head. "Nope. He's used to my being gone in the summer. I've always spent my summers with Mom's parents in Winthrop. Know where that is?"

I thought for a minute. "Maybe. Is it a real little farming town, over near the Vermont border?"

"That's right. Thomas said your dad had taken the family there on one of his famous Sunday drives. It's really just a village. My grandparents had a big dairy farm there."

"But you're not staying with them this year?"

"Nope. Granddad died two years ago, and Gram stayed on alone. She had a couple of hired men to do the farm work, and of course I was there summers and every other school vacation I could manage."

He stopped, then went on softly, "Last winter she had a stroke and couldn't stay alone any more. She had to move into a nursing home. Sometime when I have a day off I'm going to drive over and see her. She and Granddad were the ones who first took me to church." He looked out at the mountains without seeming to really see them.

I knew it was time to be heading back, but I wanted to keep him talking. "So your grandparents were . . . Christians?" I asked.

"Yes, and they always took me to church with them."

"So you only went to church in the summers?" I asked.

"Well, no. The Lord worked it out so I could go all year round. There's a Bible-preaching church just a few blocks away from us in Bayport. Dad doesn't care if I go, as long as I can get there on my own. I usually walk."

"Do you think *your* life has changed?" I asked him.

"Getting back to your question about Thomas, right? Sure I do. Because of the divorce, I was a confused kid when I accepted Christ that first summer. But it's helped me to know that God is always with me and is working everything out for my good. I want to make my life count for Him. There've been lots of changes in my life. In Thomas's too."

"Oh, I guess so," I said.

Steve stood up and stretched. "We can talk while we're walking, can't we? Your folks will be expecting us back."

"So will Thomas," I couldn't help adding. We walked in silence for a while, and I could tell he was thinking about Thomas.

"You're partly right, Liz," he said finally. "Sometimes Thomas does tend to take charge. I think he's got a lot of organizational ability. It must be tough to sit on the sidelines and see things that need to be done, yet not be able to do them. So he tells other people what to do. You have to remember that even though he's a Christian, Thomas still has the old nature he was born with. All his old personality traits, including the ones that bother you, are still there."

"I never thought about that," I admitted.

"It's true," he said. "And Satan loves it when Christians forget to pray or try to take care of matters in their own strength. Because then their old nature is what everybody sees."

I'd been so intent on what he was saying, I hadn't even noticed we were nearly home. "Thanks," I said. "I think I understand a little better now."

He smiled. "You're welcome. And Liz, don't forget that Thomas just has your good in mind. He wants so badly for you to know the Lord like he does that sometimes he sort of jumps the gun and tries to push things along himself. He prays for you every day, you know."

"Yes, I know. But why—" To my dismay, my eyes filled with angry tears. "—Why can't he just be happy with me the way I am?"

Steve held the screen door open for me. "Because he loves you, Liz."

I fled to the bathroom to pull myself together, and Steve disappeared, presumably in search of Thomas. Probably going to fill him in on the evening, I thought.

Washing my face with lots of cold water helped. As I leaned against the sink I thought about Thomas; now I understood him a little better. But I wouldn't let the events of the day weaken my resolve not to return to school. Feeling fortified, I opened the bathroom door and headed for the stairs. Might as well go to bed; I could read for a while. I didn't feel like facing either Steve Todd or the family, and especially not Thomas!

But Mom heard the creak of the door. "Liz?" she called from the office. "Were you on your way to bed, dear?"

Reluctantly, I went in. She wasn't actually working, just kind of pushing a pencil around, though the cover was off the adding machine and there was a ledger open on the desk in front of her.

"I thought I would go up, Mom. I'm sort of tired."

Mom sighed. "I wanted to talk to you about what the doctor said. I thought this would be a good time, since Thomas is busy with Steve." Her voice sort of trailed off.

"Oh, go ahead," I said. "We all know about Thomas's famous supersonic hearing."

I knew I sounded harsh and uncaring; that Mom might have preferred a rush of tears and a heart-to-heart talk, but I couldn't—simply couldn't—give in. If I ever started to really cry, I was afraid I'd never stop. Stubbornly, I remained standing, though I knew it would make it easier for Mom if I sat down.

She frowned thoughtfully. "I can't remember if I wrote you, Liz, about these spells of coughing that Thomas has had. It's only happened a couple of times before, but it shook your father and me up considerably. I did intend to write you about it, but I think Thomas didn't want me to bother you."

I could reply to this truthfully, at least. "No, Mom, you didn't tell me about it. I knew nothing about the problem until today."

She continued to doodle with her pencil. "We didn't know much about it ourselves. We'd told Dr. King, of course, at Thomas's last checkup. The coughing just seemed to start out of nowhere, and sometimes it'd clear up right away and sometimes it wouldn't. There didn't seem to be much rhyme or reason to it."

"So it's nothing serious?" I asked.

"Probably not, but with muscular dystrophy you always have to keep an eye on respiratory problems. In most cases that's what . . . what . . ."

"Finishes them off?" I asked, and immediately wished I hadn't. When would I learn to think before I spoke?

Mom winced; she glanced at the slightly open door. "That's not exactly the way I would have put it, but yes, respiratory problems often lead to death in these cases. Oh, and, one more thing, Liz."

Here it came. "What?" I just wanted to get it over with.

"It's just that Dr. King is beginning to think there may be some connection between what Thomas eats or drinks after these attacks and how long the attacks last. He says that perhaps drinking milk, or eating other dairy products like ice cream may prolong the coughing by sort of coating Thomas's throat."

"Oh, no! The milk shake I gave him only made matters worse!" I felt awful.

"Well," Mom said cautiously, "it probably didn't help much. I just wanted to tell you it might cause problems, so that if Thomas ever has another spell when you're here alone with him, you could remember to give him water or juice—anything but milk!"

"That's easy enough," I said. "Anything else?"

"No, I don't think so. Tomorrow, if you have a chance, you might pass the information on to Steve. He probably ought to know. And I've just called Mary Rose. She was quite concerned."

"I'm sure," I said, because it seemed like the thing to say. "Well, good night." And I slipped out of the office and up the stairs without seeing or speaking to anyone else.

Chapter Nine

The next few weeks went by in a blur. Every day was packed with activity: picking strawberries, working in the garden, helping with housework, swimming in the Fox River, baby-sitting my nephew, Noah, playing badminton, and helping out in the hay field and at the barn. I saw Steve Todd every day, but our relationship was casual. The conversation on the stone wall might never have taken place. Thomas hadn't mentioned school again, and he hadn't had any more coughing fits. No one else had brought up the subject of school, either, and the whole situation was beginning to get on my nerves.

If someone asked me, I'd have said I'd welcome anything that would bring matters to the surface. But no one asked me, and I would never have chosen the way it happened when it finally did.

One day in the middle of July, Mary Rose asked me to baby-sit Noah at her house. Roger was going to be busy at the farm, and she had a dental appointment.

"The perfect way to spend a hot, sticky afternoon," she said. "Glued to the dentist's chair! I know Mom is horrendously busy with book work," she went on, "so it would be much better if you came up here. Want me to come get you?"

"No problem," I said. "I don't mind walking."

So Noah and I had a fun afternoon. I filled his little wading pool and watched him while he splashed in it; that tired him out so much that he willingly took a nap. While he slept, I made a lemon chiffon pie for their supper and folded a basketful of clean towels.

Mary Rose came home while I was stacking them in the linen closet. "Aren't you sweet! You know, Liz," she said, "you've really grown up a lot this summer. You sure don't have much in common anymore with those spoiled brats at Foxville High."

I hadn't thought about that angle at all. But it suddenly hit me that she was right. I didn't know why; maybe the seriousness of Thomas's situation had affected me more than I knew. When I'd seen some of my old friends at the Fourth of July fireworks, I'd been surprised at how immature they seemed. It was a bit discouraging because I still planned to go back to public school in the fall, and who would I have for friends? The old friends didn't fit me anymore, and the achievers stuck together and wouldn't accept anyone new—especially someone they'd already branded as a troublemaker and a misfit. But I didn't belong at Mountainside Christian either, and I had no intention of going back there. So what was I going to do?

Mary Rose was speaking to me, I realized. ". . . sure you don't want me to give you a ride home?"

"Oh, no," I said. "You've had a tough afternoon. Why don't you put your feet up, and read, or do some embroidery or something while His Highness is still napping."

I started down the road, considering this new problem that Mary Rose had presented me with. It was still hot and sticky, and the mosquitoes were persistent here on the tree-lined dirt road, but I felt as if the miles I had to walk wouldn't give me nearly the amount of time I needed.

Several cars and trucks whizzed by, and a siren wailed far off in the distance, but I didn't look up. I ambled along, trying to order my thoughts. First and foremost, I didn't want to go back to Mountainside. Reason: it just wasn't me. I didn't belong there; it was for aspiring evangelists, pastors, missionaries, and musicians.

I had no intention of fitting into any of those categories, and nothing, but nothing, would ever force me to!

Second, I wanted to attend school somewhere else, preferably here in Foxville where I'd be near my family and the farm.

Third, my old friends seemed different—younger and sillier—not at all like the daring, sophisticated crowd I remembered.

Fourth, the other kids in school would not be likely to accept me. And I didn't have much in common with them, either.

Conclusion: I didn't fit anywhere. I was destined to be lonely wherever I went to school.

From somewhere inside me a voice, unbidden and unwanted, murmured, "Well, if you're going to be lonely wherever you are, why not just go back to Mountainside and please your family?"

"Because," I retorted, "I want to be my *own person!*" Then I sighed. "So what if I can't seem to figure out what that is?"

I saw to my astonishment that I was approaching the farm lane. And I was no closer to a solution than I'd been when I walked out of my sister's driveway.

As I got closer to the house, I narrowed my eyes against the hazy sunshine. I thought I could just make out a figure sitting on the ramp that led to the front door. Steve Todd! What was he doing there?

"What's going on?" I called. My throat seemed very dry all of a sudden, and not just from my hot, dusty hike.

Steve jumped to his feet and came to meet me. "Liz," he said gently, "there's been a little trouble here."

"Thomas!" I said instantly.

He nodded. "He's had another coughing spell, and this time he couldn't seem to snap out of it. The ambulance just left to take him to the hospital. He's . . . well, he's unconscious. It doesn't look good, Liz."

"Well, what are we standing around here for? We ought to be heading for the hospital this very minute!"

"We'll go in a couple of seconds," he said. "Roger went home to tell Mary Rose. He'll stay there with Noah so she can go to the hospital. She should be coming right along."

Sure enough, here came their rattletrap old car, with Mary Rose at the wheel. She jerked to a stop. My sister is not a great driver under the best of conditions, and right now she was definitely shaken. I was too, I realized, as I grabbed at the door handle with fingers that seemed to have gone numb.

Steve came to my rescue, opening the door for me. Then he leaned across to speak to Mary Rose. "Want me to drive?" he asked.

She nodded wordlessly, and they changed places. Then she found her voice. "S—Steve," she stammered, "before we leave, would you pray?"

I know Steve noticed my restlessness, but after hesitating a couple of seconds, he bowed his head. "Lord, we don't know what's going on with Thomas. We love him so much, Lord . . . we don't want to lose him. But You know all about it. You've promised to work everything together for good. Please, have Your will and way in Thomas's life. And comfort his mom and dad right now. And Lord, if it's Your will, help us to get hold of Pastor Nelson soon, so he can help the family. In Jesus' name, Amen."

As Steve put the car in gear, Mary Rose asked, "You've tried to call Pastor, then?"

"I've tried a couple of times, but there's no answer. I'll try again from the hospital."

No one spoke for the rest of the short trip. We parked the car, then hurried into the hospital. Steve stopped at the phone booth in the lobby while Mary Rose and I went on to the waiting area in the emergency room.

We sat there for what seemed like hours. Mary Rose paged listlessly through magazines while I sat tensely on the edge of my plastic chair. Some minor emergencies came and went, but I saw nothing of Thomas or my parents. The nurse on duty seemed busy, so I didn't want to ask.

Once Steve came in to say that he still couldn't reach the Nelsons by phone, but he thought he'd drive over to the parsonage. "They might be outdoors," he suggested.

Mary Rose agreed, and Steve left. I looked at Mary Rose. She had put her magazine aside and was sitting relaxed, her eyes closed. What a time to sleep! I thought. Then I realized she was praying.

I hope God is listening, I thought. But He and Mary Rose are surely on speaking terms, after all. I stared down at my feet, and the minutes inched by.

We were still sitting like that when a soft voice asked, "Mary Rose?"

We both jumped, and the owner of the voice—an attractive girl in white with dark auburn hair and deep brown eyes—slid into the chair next to my sister.

"You probably don't remember me," the girl said.

Mary Rose looked at her thoughtfully, then with dawning recognition. "Susan Greene! I haven't seen you since Typing I days!"

The girl smiled. "That's right! Mary Rose, I was here when they brought Thomas in this afternoon, and I just wanted to say . . . well, how sorry I am. You know, it was really Thomas who helped me decide on a career in medicine. At first I was interested in physical therapy—that was mostly because of Thomas—but I became a medical secretary in the end. I love it."

"Mom and Dad will be pleased to hear that, I know," Mary Rose said. "Have you seen them anywhere around?"

"Not recently, but I could probably find them for you. I'm sure you'd rather wait with them."

We agreed that we would, and Susan hurried off in search of someone who would know. She was back right away.

"Follow me." She led us down a corridor and tapped gently on a door. "Right in here."

"Thanks," said Mary Rose. "And, Sue, did you happen to see the young man who came in with us? Tall, with dark hair and glasses?" At Sue's nod, she went on. "When he comes back, will you tell him where we are? He's a good friend, and Mom and Dad would want him here."

"I'll be glad to," the girl replied, and turned back down the corridor.

And then we were alone with my parents. They looked up eagerly when the door opened; I guess they were probably expecting a doctor to be bringing them word or something. Mom's face looked terrible—white and drawn; her hands were clasped tensely in her lap. But Dad was worse; the tears were falling steadily, and he was trying to wipe them away with his big red bandanna handkerchief.

Mary Rose rushed to his side. "Oh, Dad—Dad, please don't feel so bad! I can't tell you that everything will be all right, because I don't know that. But Dad, we know the Lord, and He *does* know. Roger's home praying, and Steve's gone looking for the pastor. We can't seem to reach him by phone."

She was babbling, I thought, but it was better than that awful, silent agony we'd walked in on. I patted Mom's shoulder awkwardly and wished I could think of something to say. "Tell them about that girl in the waiting room," I finally said.

So Mary Rose told them all about Susan Greene and how Thomas had influenced her choice of a career; then she conveyed the girl's message of sympathy. That sort of broke the tension as Mom tried to puzzle out who Sue's parents were and where they lived. Even Dad seemed able to concentrate on what we were saying and was dry eyed again.

Then Mary Rose asked very gently, "How *is* Thomas?"

Mom looked down at her hands in her lap. "They whisked him off somewhere and were trying to revive him, last we knew. We haven't seen him since."

Dad spoke up. "Dr. King said he'll let us know, the minute there's anything to tell." His voice trembled, but he was no longer the weeping stranger we'd seen from the doorway.

There was a tap on the door, and this time we all looked up expectantly. But instead of Dr. King, Steve Todd stood there.

"Come in, Steve," said Mom. "You may as well wait with us. We're expecting the doctor to give us a report as soon as he can. Did you find Pastor Nelson?"

Steve came into the room and sank into a chair. "Not exactly. I left a note on the parsonage door and one at the church. One of the deacons was there mowing the lawn. He suggested we could get in touch with one of the elders. So I've called Mr. Davis—"

"Well, you've done all you can," Mom told him comfortingly. "All we can do now is wait and pray."

There was another soft knock on the door, and Dr. King came in. I'd forgotten how young he looked; maybe it was his wavy dark hair.

"Thomas is alive," he said, and I know we all breathed more easily. "But," Dr. King continued, "he's not in very good shape. Basically, he's in a coma. We don't know if he'll come out of it or how much brain damage there's been. I know this sounds negative and discouraging, but you have to know. He could die at any time, or he could go on like this indefinitely." He paused before continuing. "I think that because Thomas looked so well, we all thought he'd live for a long time yet. In reality, he's already outlived most victims of this type of muscular dystrophy. He could have died any time in the last few years. Do any of you have any questions?"

Mom took a deep breath. "When can we see him?" she asked.

"You and your husband should be able to see him quite soon. He's just been taken up to the intensive care unit, and, as soon as they get him all settled in, you'll be notified. The rest of you"—his gaze included me, Steve, and Mary Rose—"may as well go on home for now. If his condition stabilizes, you can see him later tonight. Okay?"

I was relieved that we'd be able to go. But Mom had other ideas.

Chapter Ten

"Shouldn't his sisters see him before they leave, Doctor?" she asked. "If he should . . . go, they'll want to have . . . well, said good-by."

Dr. King considered. "It's up to you, Mrs. Williamson, but I'd say no. If Thomas should come to, he'll want to see you and your husband. Even now, he may possibly hear and recognize your voices and be comforted by that. It would be better if you two have some time alone with him first, and other family members could come in later tonight. Then you can prepare them for the somewhat disturbing sight of Thomas connected to various tubes, gauges, and bottles."

Mom and Dad both nodded, and after hugging them once more we left the hospital and headed home.

"Drop me at the barn, okay?" Steve suggested to Mary Rose. "I'll do the chores tonight."

"Let me help," I pleaded. "I've got to do something strenuous or burst."

"Good idea," said Mary Rose. "When you've finished, why don't you both come on up to the house for supper? If I know Roger, he's whipped up some sort of meal, and I noticed that a yummy looking pie had magically appeared in our refrigerator."

We agreed to do that, and she left us at the barn. It was sort of comforting to fall into the standard routine of caring for the animals. Steve and I didn't say much to each other, just murmuring to the cattle and horses as we worked, but the silence was soothing after the tension of the hospital. I was still badly shaken, but for now I was content with this peaceful numbness. Soon enough, I'd have to face facts.

Even after Steve had closed the barn doors and we were chugging toward Mary Rose's in the farm pickup, I didn't have much to say. Steve was quiet too, but as we pulled into the driveway, he spoke up.

"Don't forget, kids are very sensitive. It's okay to let Noah see you're concerned, but don't go to pieces if you can help it."

The words were spoken out of concern for Noah, I knew, but they came across as harsh and critical. I found myself replying in kind. "I'm perfectly well aware of that, Stephen Todd! Do you think I'm an absolute idiot?"

He smiled at that. "I don't know what I think, Liz. I'm sorry. Let's forget it and go have supper. I'm starved, aren't you?"

I hadn't thought I was, but as we stepped onto the porch and were greeted with the aroma of grilled hamburgers, I was suddenly ravenous. Roger came around the corner waving a spatula.

"Greetings! Noah and I decided to cook out. Everything's ready, so come on back and find a seat."

The hamburgers, potato salad, and sliced ripe tomatoes tasted marvelous. I felt almost guilty to be enjoying the food so much, knowing what might be going on at the hospital.

We didn't talk much during the meal. We were all so hungry that at first we kept busy eating, and of course we were trying to act fairly normal for Noah's sake. Finally he wandered off to play with his sand toys, and Mary Rose went inside and got the pie.

"What should we do about going back to the hospital?" she asked. "I know we all want to go, but we can't, unless we take Noah with us. And I don't really want to have to cope with him running around the waiting room."

"No problem," Steve said. "You and Roger go first. Liz and I will do up the dishes and look after Noah. Then, when you come back, we'll go."

Everyone agreed to that; they also said that the pie was fantastic. "Liz, you ought to open a restaurant," groaned Roger. "You'd do a great business at first; at least until your customers learned that they couldn't get up from the table after one of your meals."

"I'll open one," I said, "when you agree to go into business with me. You could be in charge of cremating all the hamburgers."

Later, when they had gone and I was washing the dishes, Steve asked, "What do you want to do with your life, Liz? I'm not taking Roger's restaurant idea seriously, but you could open a bakery someday, or do catering, maybe." He picked up a dishtowel. "You know, I got to thinking about that talk we had. I was so busy telling you the story of my life, I never got around to asking about your plans for the future."

I sighed and swished the water in the sink. "I don't know, really. I keep changing my mind."

"Well, that's not so strange. I think most kids our age do the same thing."

"Yeah, but *they* change their minds about concrete things. You know, they might want to be a cowboy at three years old, a fireman at five, a race car driver at eight, a doctor at ten—that kind of thing."

"But not you, huh?"

"Nope. Not me. If you'd asked me that question a year ago, I would've said that I wanted to be the exact opposite of whatever convention expected of me. If you'd asked me a month ago, or even this morning, I'd have said, 'I just want to be myself—whoever that is.' But now I think that what I'd really like would be for everything in my life to stay forever the way it's been this summer. Up to now."

He smiled sympathetically. "But that can't happen, you know. Not in real life."

"If I hadn't realized that before, I know it now beyond any doubt," I said shakily. "Oh, Steve, it's so scary not knowing what's going to happen to Thomas—or to any of us!"

The room grew quiet. Then Steve said, "I remember an old Sunday school song. The words went something like, 'I know who holds the future, and I know who holds my hand.' It's true, none of us do know what the future holds. But that doesn't scare me. I'm a child of the very same God who created the universe. I know He'll do what's best for me."

The look in his eyes almost undid me, but then I remembered something he had apparently forgotten—Thomas in the hospital, wired to tubes and bottles.

"How can you say that?" I demanded. "How can you say that God does what's best for those who love Him, when Thomas is lying in a coma? If anybody loves God, it's Thomas. So how could God do this to him? If that's a sample of God's love, it's not for me!"

I'd forgotten Noah, who'd been playing with his miniature farm set in the living room. Now he came into the kitchen, waving a tiny red tractor at me.

"Don't yell, Aunt Wiz! Isn't nice!"

I began to laugh. "Scolded by a two-year-old! I guess it serves me right. Sorry, Steve."

He smiled as he wiped the last dish and hung up his towel, but it seemed like his smile was a pitying one. For me?

Noah was capering toward the door, shouting, "Mommy! Daddy!" So I assumed his parents were back. Soon enough, they came in and collapsed into kitchen chairs.

I looked at their tense faces. "Is he worse?"

Roger shook his head. "No change." He sighed deeply. "It's just . . . oh, I feel so bad for your folks, Liz. Their life has centered on Thomas all these years. This is so hard for them! It's awful for anyone to lose a child. But most people who lose grown children aren't this close to them. Your parents have had to plan everything around Thomas; he's lived at home all his life, and they've shared a lot. Imagine being that close to someone for years and then to have him snatched away from you. They're going to need plenty of prayer."

This long and rambling speech, I knew, was not typical of Roger. He tended to think things out carefully and weigh his words before speaking. I could only conclude that he was upset, and I didn't blame him, but something he said pricked me.

"You talk as if he's already dead!" I blurted out.

Noah, catching the gist of our conversation, immediately burst into noisy tears. Mary Rose, giving me a now-look-what-you've-done glance, scooped him up and carried him off.

"We'd planned to tell him about this a little more gently," Roger said. "We don't want to scare him because we want to take him in to see Thomas, if we can. You know how Thomas dotes on Noah."

I certainly did, and I felt terrible that my outburst might have spoiled their plans for handling the situation. "I'm sorry." I seemed to be apologizing all over the place tonight. I turned to Steve. "Time we were leaving, don't you think?"

"No hurry," Roger told us. "We can visit any time in intensive care, even after regular visiting hours."

"Still," I said, "I'd like to get going."

Steve followed me out the door, calling his thanks to Roger for the meal. He seemed his usual friendly self, but when we were seated in the truck, he didn't put the key into the ignition but sat swinging it between his fingers. And he didn't look friendly anymore. He looked just plain angry.

"What's the matter with you?" he asked. "Do you think you've done Noah any good with those childish outbursts?" He looked at me, his expression deadly serious. "Are you going to do the same thing at the hospital? Because if you are, I'm not so sure I want to take you there."

I opened my mouth, but Steve wasn't finished. He took a deep breath, as if to calm himself down, and went on.

"Please, I know this is hard for you, but your attitude will only make matters worse for your parents. You've got to start thinking of others' feelings as well as your own."

I sat there, biting my lip to hold back the tears that were close to the surface.

"I won't upset them. I promise," I finally said. "I only want to see Thomas . . . and I promise that if . . . if I feel like doing or saying something upsetting, I'll just . . . go out to the truck and wait for you. Please take me there. I'll let you do all the talking."

He smiled then, a tiny smile, but a smile nonetheless. "Okay," he said. "And I'm sorry I lost my temper. It's one of my besetting sins. Now, let's go."

Chapter Eleven

I guess nobody, no matter what they think, is ever really prepared to go through the door of an intensive care unit and see a loved one hooked up to life supports. With all the talk about gauges and dials, I thought I knew what to expect. But when the person in the bed became Thomas, it took every ounce of self-control I possessed to keep from bursting into sobs.

And if the sight of Thomas, with tubes in his nose and mouth, had shaken me, looking at my parents was even worse. Dad, head bowed, sat at one side of the bed in a straight chair. Mom sat in a rocking chair on Thomas's other side, stroking his hand and murmuring to him.

The silence, the warm cleanliness of the room and the sterile white bedding, the gentle rhythm of the respirator and other machines all combined to create a peaceful cocoon around Thomas.

Mom glanced up. "Here are Liz and Steve," she said softly. "They're here to see you, Thomas."

"Can he hear you?" I whispered. Thomas's eyes were closed, and he seemed to be asleep.

Dad got up then. "Come on down the hall with me, and I'll fill you in." He folded up his reading glasses, stuck the case in his pocket, and handed Mom his Bible.

We followed him to a cheerful room furnished with couches, chairs, and a television set—the solarium.

Dad eased himself into a chair and motioned to Steve and me to sit too. "We don't know whether Thomas can hear us or not," he began. "But Dr. King says we should assume that he can. To come out of this coma, Thomas needs stimulation—that is, we need to touch him and speak to him. But we won't talk about his condition in front of him."

Steve glanced at me out of the corner of his eye. He still doesn't trust me, I thought. He's sure that if I'm allowed to see Thomas, I'll manage to upset him somehow. Well, I'll show him!

Outwardly, I maintained a calm gaze as I listened to Dad continue speaking. "It could be a long haul, kids, or . . . the end could come quickly. Right now, we don't know. As I see it, what we've got to do is just trust the Lord and pray for His will to be worked out in all of our lives, not just Thomas's."

From the doorway of the solarium came a quiet "I agree," and Pastor and Mrs. Nelson walked in.

"I'm terribly sorry that I wasn't here when you needed me," Pastor Nelson said, "but I know the Lord sustained you. That's obvious, from what you were telling these young people when we came in."

"It was all His doing, Pastor," Dad replied. "I was pretty shaken up at first, but now I've been able to spend some time with the Lord. He has His reasons, and someday we'll understand all that's happening—in glory, if not here."

Pastor Nelson nodded, and Mrs. Nelson turned to me. "Have you seen him yet, Liz?" She patted my shoulder comfortingly.

"Just for a minute," I said stiffly. "Dad wanted to fill us in on a few things first."

"Oh, of course," she murmured. I thought she wanted to say something more, but she just smiled and touched my shoulder again.

Dad got to his feet and motioned us toward the door. "Why don't we go back and see how Thomas is doing? Pastor, I'm sure you'll understand that Liz is anxious to get in and see him. She and Steve have been waiting a long time. You won't mind a short wait, will you?"

The Nelsons said they had plenty of time, so Dad went into the ICU to check with Mom. He came out and said quietly, "There's no change. You can go on in."

The room was so quiet I felt that I should tiptoe. It was like being in a hushed, thickly carpeted church, or the nursery of a sleeping baby. Mom still sat by the bedside, stroking his hand.

"Here are Liz and Steve again, Thomas. I told you they'd be back. I'm going to go get a cup of coffee now, while they visit with you. I'll be right back, so don't worry."

"The Nelsons are here," I told Mom.

"Oh, good!" She glanced at Thomas. "Just go ahead and talk to him, both of you. Don't be shy." She went out.

I hadn't thought I could ever be shy with Thomas, but looking at his peaceful face, I couldn't think of one word to say.

As usual, Steve came to the rescue. He went around to the other side of the bed and picked up Thomas's hand. "Hi, Thomas old boy, how're you feeling tonight? Pretty tired, are you? I had a rough day myself; it's hot out in the hay field, so you sweat, and everything sticks to you. Look close, and you might even see some chaff on my arms. I haven't had a chance to clean up yet. This harebrained sister of yours has had me on the run all evening."

He looked at me. His eyes said clearly, "Your turn."

I tried. "Listen to him!" I said lightly. "Trying to make you feel sorry for him! Well, we've been doing a lot more than driving around; we had a cookout with Roger and Mary Rose. . . ."

I broke off, looking down at the unresponsive features. I could just hear him saying, "Sure, sure, tell me about it, Lizard. You probably ate more than Steve did. You, with the famous appetite!"

But he *wasn't* answering, and I had to wonder if he ever would again. Right at the moment, I would have given a lot even to hear him teasing me. Why didn't Mom come back?

Steve seemed to read my mind, because he leaned forward and picked up Thomas's hand again while he talked softly. He kept it up until Mom came in with Pastor Nelson. I felt like crying, but I remembered my promise to Steve, and my unspoken promise to Mom and Dad. I clenched my hands until little red crescents appeared in the palms.

At the sight of Mom and the pastor, Steve got up. He patted Thomas's shoulder and said, "Time for me and Liz to go now, buddy. You've got more company here now, and we'll see you tomorrow, okay?"

I touched Thomas's hand and added, "Bye now, Thomas. I'll come again tomorrow."

Mom motioned for me to kiss him, but I just couldn't. I'd break down for sure if I did. I shook my head hurriedly, hoping she'd understand, but right away I could see that she didn't. I just said, "Good night, Mom," and dashed out.

Behind me, I could see Steve taking her hand and saying he'd be praying for her and Dad. That's right, I thought. He always knows exactly what to say.

When we reached the truck again, though, I was glad I hadn't made any comments about Steve's way with words. He looked at me, silently, and I could see tears in his eyes.

Finally he said, "I'm not going to ask, 'Why Thomas?' I know God has a purpose in this. But if it's hitting me this hard, when I've only known Thomas a short time, it has to be so much worse for your family. I just want to say that if there's anything I can do to help, I will. I know Mr. Evans will understand."

"That's nice of you, Steve," I said, "but I think you've done an awful lot already. Having you in there with me tonight meant more than I can say. I could never have done it alone."

He nodded as he started the truck. Over the roar of the motor, I thought I heard him mutter something like, "You don't have to do anything alone," but I couldn't be sure.

On the way home, we discussed where I'd spend the night. Steve was all for taking me back to Mary Rose's, figuring that Mom and Dad would be quite late. But I held out for going back to the farm. I wanted to be there when they got home, so I'd know how Thomas was doing, and maybe fix them a snack or something.

After Steve had gone, I puttered around the house straightening things up. Everything was just as it had been when they rushed to the hospital, and I didn't want Mom coming home to the reminders of it all. Then I fixed a plate of crackers and cheese, filled the teakettle, and sat down with a book to wait.

But I couldn't concentrate. The minutes ticked by. It was almost midnight. I wondered what Steve was doing. Sleeping, probably, or praying. He had the strongest faith of anyone I'd ever met. I wondered if he ever prayed for me. Somehow, the thought didn't bother me as much as it once would have. I almost envied Steve his faith in God.

Then I straightened up and squared my shoulders. What are you talking about? I scolded myself. You're just shaken up. You don't seriously think it was God who let this happen to Thomas, do you? And you can't really believe that Steve's prayers, or anyone else's, can make a difference in the outcome. Don't be ridiculous!

I picked up my book again, and this time my eyes began to close. I was awakened by Mom shaking me.

"Liz . . . Liz . . . wake up, dear. It's after midnight, and you should get to bed. You should have gone long before now."

I struggled to wake up. "I know, Mom, . . . but I wanted to hear . . . how Thomas is."

"Just the same, dear. Well, there's a very slight change. Don't get your hopes up, now, but just before we left, it seemed like his eyelashes were beginning to flutter a bit. As if he was trying to open his eyes! The nurses said it might not mean anything. But, oh, if he opens his eyes, I'll know it was the Lord's doing!"

I rubbed my own eyes. "Well, that's something. Did you and Dad find the cheese and crackers?"

"I did," mumbled Dad from the kitchen. "Thanks, honey."

"You're welcome," I called sleepily. "Well, good night. See you in the morning."

I hurried upstairs before they could involve me in teary hugs—Mom's specialty—or a family prayer time—Dad's department. I love my family very much and don't usually find it hard to show them that. But I absolutely despise sticky sentimentality. The further away I could stay from that, the happier I'd be!

It's funny. Even as a little kid, when I hurt myself, I'd get over it faster if no one showed me any sympathy. But give me a hug, and the floodgates would open! Underwater band concert, Thomas used to call my sobs.

I didn't expect to go to sleep right away, so I picked up my book again, but I felt myself falling asleep before I was halfway through the page.

Chapter Twelve

I didn't wake until Mom called me the next morning. When I dragged myself into the dining room, she greeted me with a bright smile. "Good news, Liz!"

"Really?" I blinked the sleep out of my eyes and tried to look awake.

"Yes! I called the hospital just after seven so I could speak to one of the night nurses. She tells me Thomas's eyes are open, and he seems quite alert!"

"Is he talking?" I asked breathlessly.

"Not yet, but she said he definitely seems to be aware of his surroundings. Isn't that wonderful? The Lord is so good to us!"

"That's *great!*" I busied myself pouring corn flakes into a bowl, slicing a banana on top of the cereal, getting some milk. "Are you going down to the hospital right away?"

"Just as soon as Dad finishes morning chores. We're taking a lunch, and we'll spend the day there." She was pouring hot coffee into Dad's big stainless steel Thermos as she spoke. "And I need to talk to you, Liz, about your responsibilities here at home."

I'd been about to pour milk over my cereal, but I put the jug back on the counter. Mom could take fifteen minutes to get out what other people could say in five. She'd been a schoolteacher before she married Dad, so I figured all this patient explaining was a holdover from those days. "Okay," I said. "Fire when ready."

"Oh, Liz! Must you be so flippant?" But a tiny smile lurked at the corner of her mouth, so I knew she wasn't totally disgusted with me.

"It's just this," she went on. "Dad and I feel we should spend most of our time at the hospital. We think we should both be there for Thomas, and we want to be available for Dr. King, anytime he might need to speak with us."

"Sounds like a good idea."

"Well, Dad and I talked for hours last night. We just don't know how long Thomas may be hospitalized, but we had to make some sort of plan. Dad will keep on doing the morning chores as usual, since he's used to getting up early. We'd be in the way if we arrived at the hospital much before eight, anyway."

"So, will Roger be handling evening chores and the other farm work?" I asked.

"Roger and Steve will be doing that. Mr. Evans has his hay all in now, and he's told us we can have Steve's help just as long as we need him. Wasn't that kind?"

"It sure was, but that means you won't need me to help with the chores. What did you have in mind for me?"

Mom took a deep breath. "It won't be easy, Liz, but I think you can do it. You see, my being away from home every day also means I'm not in the office. The bookwork has to be done; it can't wait just because I have to be somewhere else."

I stared at her in horror, and she smiled before replying.

"No, Liz, I don't plan for you to do the bookkeeping! Remember, Mary Rose took some accounting courses in high school, and she's helped me out over the years. She's offered to take over the office work. She thinks she can fit in some housework and laundry too, if—and this is a big 'if'—you'd be willing to look after Noah and fix whatever meals are needed."

"Well, sure," I said slowly. "I'd be glad to, but that doesn't seem like very much to do. It's fun to take care of Noah, and you know cooking is almost like breathing for me. Isn't there something more I could do?"

"Liz, if you can do all that, it'll be all you *can* do, believe me. Children have fussy days. Sometimes they get sick. Caring for a child, day in and day out, is very different from baby-sitting once in a while. And as for the cooking, even experienced cooks find it challenging to plan meals that can be eaten at odd hours."

"Will I have time to visit Thomas?" I asked.

"Yes, we've thought of that too. Evenings will be Roger and Mary Rose's time to visit, but in the afternoons when Noah is taking his nap, you'll have a free hour or two to spend with Thomas. Steve can drive you there. Good enough?"

"Fine," I answered. It was a lot to take in so quickly.

"That's that, then," she said. "Oh, here's Dad. Good; as soon as he changes, we'll be off. Mary Rose is coming at ten; that'll give you a good couple of hours to plan your day." She hurried off to brush her teeth.

I poured my milk and some orange juice, then sank into a chair, trying to order my thoughts. It would be important to plan good meals each evening that Mom and Dad could share. The noon meal was usually quite simple, so I'd really only have to concentrate on one meal a day. An idea struck me, and I got up to explore the refrigerator and canned goods shelves.

Yes, the cupboard was definitely growing bare. I'd have to make a trip to the supermarket, and soon! Somehow I'd fit that into my plans.

My corn flakes grew mushy as I contemplated my new job. Noah would also be a challenge because, of course, Mary Rose had been away each time I'd taken care of him before. This time, she would be only too available, and I could see that keeping him out of the office would be a full-time activity.

Noah made my worst fears come true. I distracted him with the open toy box—a treat that was usually forbidden. I tried play dough, the sandpile, and finally, in desperation, cookies—all to no avail. He'd play for a few minutes, then it was back to the office door to engage Mama in conversation. When I got firm and removed him bodily, he screamed as if someone had tried to murder him. My sunshiny nephew was fast becoming an insufferable little brat!

If Mom were here, I thought, she'd have all sorts of excuses for him: he's tired, he senses the tension in the air, you name it. Dad wouldn't be quite so tolerant. And if Roger had heard those screams, well . . .

I decided to try removing Noah from Mary Rose's orbit; he wasn't doing much for her concentration. I scooped him up and carried him outside, screaming all the way. That is, Noah was screaming. I wasn't, but I felt like it.

"Noah," I coaxed, "let's go look at the cows." He quieted down a little, sobbing more softly now. The best strategy, I decided, was to keep him outdoors as much as possible. As we headed for the barnyard and the pasture gate, I mentally planned the afternoon's activities. Lunch, of course, and then a good long walk until nap time. Maybe the walk would tire him so much that he'd sleep the rest of the afternoon.

As we watched the black-and-white cows peacefully grazing, Noah's sobs subsided. He was still heaving and twitching from his temper tantrum, but he reached out a chubby hand and breathed, "Moo!" as a cow came toward us curiously.

Then Roger appeared around the side of the barn. "Hi, guys!" he called. "How's it going, Liz?"

As he came closer, I knew he was going to see exactly how things had been going. And he did.

"Noah Brainerd!" he scolded. "What seems to be the problem here?"

"Well," I said, "he, well, he seems to want to be with Mary Rose all the time. She couldn't concentrate. So I thought I'd bring him outside and—"

"And he threw a fit," Roger concluded. "This can't continue, obviously. I'll handle this, Liz. Come on, Noah." He reached out for Noah, who was all smiles again. Not for long, I thought. Roger would handle the situation quite thoroughly. Then he would probably keep Noah occupied until lunch time, thus proving that he still loved him.

"Sorry about taking up your time like this, Rog," I called after him.

"Oh, it's no trouble. We need to get this settled right away, so he knows what's what. I'll service my equipment this afternoon instead. It's supposed to rain, anyway. See you at lunch, Liz."

Rain! I could have cried. There went my nice long walk with Noah. Listlessly, I went inside and began preparing lunch. During one of Noah's ten-minute periods of being good, I'd found some cold boiled potatoes in the refrigerator, cubed them, poured oil and vinegar over them, and left them to marinate. Now, I took canned tuna and home-canned green beans from the pantry shelf and concocted a Salade Nicoise of sorts. While it chilled, I baked a pan of cornbread and made some chocolate sauce to go over ice cream. People are always amazed that New England farmers seem to eat dessert at *every* meal. But they work harder than anyone else I know. Dad, Roger, and Steve are all as thin as rails and really seem to need those extra calories. Dad prefers more substantial desserts like rice pudding, or pie, but ice cream would do for today.

As usual, cooking had improved my mood. When we all gathered for lunch, I was feeling more optimistic about everything.

Mary Rose praised the meal. "That salad is simply gorgeous!"

Steve and Roger echoed her. "I don't think there are very many farmers in New Hampshire sitting down to a lunch like this one," said Roger.

It tasted pretty good too, and we were enjoying it so much we didn't even notice the darkening sky. Suddenly, an enormous crack of thunder made us all jump, and Noah started to cry. As Mary Rose hurried to soothe him, the rain began pelting down in huge drops.

"Here comes your rain, Roger," I said. And there goes my afternoon, I thought.

Chapter Thirteen

Noah had stopped fussing, and Mary Rose looked at me over his head. "Really, Liz, you did pretty well to create any kind of meal out of what was on hand. I guess Mom hasn't shopped for a while, by the look of the refrigerator."

I nodded. "I'll have to shop soon."

Unexpectedly, Steve spoke up. "Make a list, Liz, and I'll take you to the supermarket right after we finish eating. Roger won't be needing me anymore today, with this rain, will you, Rog? And let's take Noah with us. It'll be fun for him."

Mary Rose looked doubtful, but Roger was nodding. "Great idea. He'll love it, and you'll be back in plenty of time for his nap."

So it was settled. While they ate dessert, I planned and wrote furiously, and twenty minutes later we were entering the supermarket with Noah settled in a shopping cart—or a "copping shart" as he insisted on calling it.

It was funny how Steve made even grocery shopping a fun experience. The warmth of his personality seemed to spill over everything and change it. Just for the moment, I forgot that Thomas was ill, forgot I was in charge of a cranky two-year-old—forgot everything but pushing my leisurely way through the aisles, stocking up on whatever would be needed to produce a couple of weeks' worth of nourishing meals.

As we went around the market, Steve kept picking up those little sample packs of everything from cookies to detergents and adding them to the cart. "These are for me," he explained, piling them separately in one corner. "They're really an incredible bargain."

"Are they?" I asked. I'd always been taught by Mom and Mary Rose that it was more economical to buy the largest possible size of anything.

"Well, some of them really are. The cookies, for instance. If you figure it out by ounces, those small packages are a pretty good deal. The others may not be, but they're cheap, and it's a good way to try something new."

I nodded, thinking that he seemed to know a lot, even though he was so young. I wondered if he learned it all somehow or was born that way.

It was still raining when we came out of the store. Steve piled grocery bags all around my feet, since we'd had to use the truck.

"Want to take a quick run by the hospital?" he asked. "We can't stay long because of the perishable groceries, but we could go in for a few minutes."

"Okay. Maybe Noah could even look in."

"Maybe," said Steve, turning into Hospital Road. "We can ask, anyway. I wonder if there's any change."

I've noticed something about hospitals. They have a certain—well, not really a smell, though I've heard it described that way. It's more of an atmosphere: a clean, steamy kind of scent, like a dryer full of Noah's diapers. It's really quite nice, but it is distinctive.

As we climbed the stairs to the second floor, I wondered what we'd find. Steve, looking fairly cheerful, was carrying Noah on his shoulders, but I couldn't tell what he was thinking.

We turned the corner toward intensive care, and the first person we saw was Mom, balancing a cup of steaming coffee. I was glad to see her, because I'd dreaded having a nurse see us with Noah and maybe stopping us.

Mom, intent on her brimming Styrofoam cup, hadn't seen us yet. I couldn't help thinking how young and attractive she looked, even with all she was coping with right now. She looked up then, and her whole face seemed to glow, as if she were lit up from inside.

"Mrs. Williamson!" Steve called. "Is there good news?"

"Gam! Gam!" chirped Noah.

Somehow Mom managed to retain her grip on her coffee cup. She smiled radiantly in our direction. "Yes, there's wonderful news! Just let me take a few sips of this coffee, and I'll tell you all about it. Come on in here." She gestured toward the solarium.

We followed, and Steve knelt on the carpet and let Noah slide to the floor. The rest of us sat down, Steve rubbing his shoulders. Noah was heavy, as I had reason to know.

Mom sipped her coffee. "Mmm, that's good. It's the first thing I've really tasted in two days. All right," she said, looking into our eager faces, "here's the good news: Thomas knows us!"

I don't know what I was expecting, but I sure felt let down. It seemed like such a slight improvement.

Steve must have seen my face. "It's a big step, Liz," he said gently. "You folks must be thrilled," he added to Mom.

She pulled a crumpled tissue out of her pocket and dabbed at her eyes. "I should say so! He still can't speak, Steve, but this is almost as good. He definitely recognizes us both, and he seems to understand what we're saying. He responds by raising his eyebrows and by sort of widening his eyes."

"What does the doctor think?" asked Steve.

"Well, he's being cautious, of course. He's pleased that Thomas is so alert and responsive, but he won't actually agree that Thomas knows what we're saying. He doesn't want us to get our hopes up too much, but he says he is encouraged. Still, it doesn't mean Thomas will ever . . . come back home again." Her voice broke, and she steadied it, then continued. "But it's so much easier just to be able to talk to him and see him respond."

I jumped up. "We forgot about the ice cream!"

Steve stood up too. "That's right, we did. Uh, Mrs. Williamson, what are the chances of our seeing Thomas for just a minute before we leave?"

"Oh, of course," Mom said. "I'm sorry; I just went gabbing on, never even thinking. You must have just come from the grocery store."

She took another sip of her coffee and went on. "I'm sure it'll be fine if you just look in on Thomas. He's the only patient in intensive care right now, so it won't disturb anyone. And Dr. King thinks it would be nice for Noah to visit too."

"That's great!" Steve shouldered Noah again, and we set off down the hall.

We tiptoed into the room, and everything looked as it had the night before. Dad even sat in the same place, and he looked as if he was still praying. The difference was that his face seemed relaxed, and I could tell that his prayer was one of thanksgiving. But Thomas's eyes were closed.

Dad looked up at us. "He's almost asleep," he said. "The nurse says it's only natural; all that activity this morning was hard work for him, and it tired him out." Dad grinned up at Noah. "Well, well," he added, "just look who's here!"

All of us who'd been worried about Noah's reaction needn't have bothered. He didn't seem to find it the slightest bit strange. In fact, he just stretched out his hand toward Thomas as if he wanted to touch him. So Mom scooped Noah up and brought him closer to the bed. And, before anyone could stop him, he had leaned down and planted his rosy little lips on Thomas's cheek. Thomas's eyelids fluttered open, and he looked right at Noah. Then his mouth stretched out in what was unmistakably a smile, and he closed his eyes again.

"Now he knows everything's okay," said Steve softly, and we all nodded.

Not long afterwards, we left. "I'll read Noah to sleep while you put away the groceries," Steve offered. "You probably want to think about starting supper soon, don't you?"

He was right, of course. And I felt almost cheerful as I prepared a festive meal in honor of Thomas's improved condition. I pan-broiled some T-bone steaks from the freezer to serve with baked potatoes and a huge tossed salad. For dessert I baked Dad's favorite—lemon meringue pie.

"It's good to have the sense of taste back again," commented Dad, and I think everyone agreed. That night we all slept soundly too.

Chapter Fourteen

One day melted into the next. Everything settled into a routine of cooking, Noah-sitting, and visits to the hospital. Before I knew it, three weeks had gone by. Thomas still wasn't talking, but he was communicating pretty well. Mom and Dad spent a lot of time reading aloud to him, from the Bible as well as from his favorite books, and they played Christian music tapes for him. And they talked, oh, how they talked! It can be awfully frustrating to try to speak with someone who can't answer. But Mom insisted that he was responding to conversation, and Steve called his visits with Thomas "talking." His condition stayed pretty much the same, and he was still in intensive care.

One Thursday, Steve came in for supper and said abruptly, "Remember the time I told you about my grandmother? Think you'd like to meet her?"

Mystified, I nodded. "Sure. Were you planning to go sometime soon?"

He ran a hand through his wavy dark hair in a distracted way. "I think I ought to, Liz. Her last letter sounded . . . I don't know, it just seems like she needs some company. She really has nobody else, and I decided when I got her letter that I'd go as soon as I could. Roger can spare me tomorrow, and now that Thomas's condition is sort of stable, I feel better about leaving."

"Tomorrow? Well, I should be able to manage. I can work out a meal to prepare ahead—but oh! There's Noah. What'll I do with him?"

Steve grinned. "Oh, I told Rog it'd be no bother at all to take Noah with us. I love kids, you know."

I knew. And I also knew by now that Steve was a super Noah-sitter. He was kind, gentle, and fun-loving, but very firm. Mary Rose wasn't sure we could handle the job, but Steve talked her into it.

"But his toilet training!" she protested.

"No problem. If I can't manage to take a two-year-old to the bathroom at the right time, I'm in big trouble."

I had to smother a laugh at the way Steve got around all Mary Rose's objections. But she and Roger did insist that we take their car, which ran well and was much more roomy than the truck.

We got an early start because Steve said morning was his grandmother's best time. "She just naturally wakes up early, after all those years on a farm," he explained, "so she feels pretty good in the morning. After lunch, though, she likes a nap."

I left sandwiches and potato salad in the refrigerator for the others to eat at lunch time, and we were off.

Noah, who'd been up with the sun, fell asleep before we were five miles down the road. The sun made us all warm and drowsy, and a long, pleasant silence filled the car.

Finally Steve broke it by saying, "Maybe I should tell you a little bit about Gram, Liz. You'll like her anyway, but you'll appreciate her even more if you know something about her life."

I smiled at him encouragingly. "I'd like that."

He took a deep breath. "Most people who've met Gram wouldn't believe that she quit school after the eighth grade. She seems sort of . . . well, ladylike, and educated, and as if she'd always had money."

"Refined?" I suggested.

"I guess that comes pretty close," Steve agreed. "Anyway, she looks that way, but she had a rough childhood. Her father was sick and couldn't work, so they were really poor. Gram had to leave school when she was thirteen, and she went to work as a hired girl."

"How awful!" I said. "Go on." I was sure the story had a happy ending.

"Well, for a few years she worked for a farm family in another state," Steve said, "and she sent all her wages home. Then something happened that changed her life."

"What was it?"

He chuckled. "The oldest son of the family—his name was Will—came home from agricultural college to take over the farm. And the first thing he did was fall in love with Emily, the hired girl! That was Gram. You can imagine how his parents reacted."

I sure could. "Probably they were angry enough to disinherit him?"

"You're right. But he married Gram anyway. They moved to New Hampshire and started their own dairy farm. It was a good one too."

I remembered something then. "You told me once that your grandparents were the ones who first took you to church. Had they always been church-going people?"

"Yes and no. Granddad's family were real pious "religious" folks who didn't live their faith. But his college roommate was a Christian who really helped him to grow."

"What about your grandmother?" I asked.

"Well, Gram trusted Christ while she was working for the Ames family. And when she and Granddad got married, they decided to always put the Lord first." He paused. "Hey, doesn't that sign up ahead say Ashworth?"

We got off the interstate and drove through a sleepy riverside village, then out into farming country. The nursing home, Steve told me, was run by the state. I'd always thought of the county homes as places for people with nowhere else to go.

"Why is she here?" I asked. "Instead of, well . . . the kind of home with hairdressers, craft groups, and shopping trips?"

Steve chuckled. "She's got a mind of her own, Liz, and it's still pretty sharp. Most of her money's still tied up in the farm. She's trying to hang onto it, hoping it'll be mine someday. So she lives here, and she insists that the care is just fine."

"I'm sure it is," I said slowly. "But what about the other residents? Lots of the people in these places are either senile or retarded. They make weird noises, they dribble their food—"

"Gram says that doesn't bother her. And she believes God will use her here as a witness to those who can understand, and to the staff. You have to respect her for that."

By now, we had reached the nursing home, which was large, brick, and imposing, as all such places seem to be. Noah was fascinated by the flight of granite steps leading to the front entrance. He wanted to go back down so we could climb up again, but Steve talked him out of that by promising we'd do it on the way out.

At the reception desk, Steve checked on the number of his grandmother's room. As we walked down a long, sparkling clean corridor and passed through heavy double doors, I shivered. On both sides of us were people with every sort of disability. Some were sitting in wheelchairs; others were shuffling slowly along. They all noticed Noah, reaching out to touch him or to croon something to him. All the attention was beginning to scare the little guy, so Steve picked him up.

Finally we came to the right door. It was ajar, and Steve knocked gently.

"Come in," said a surprisingly young voice. We entered, and the woman in the chair by the window turned toward us.

"Steve!" she cried. I never could have imagined that so much gladness, so much love, could be conveyed in just one syllable.

Her hair was snow white and cut quite short so that it clustered in little curls all over her head. She wore gold-rimmed glasses, but behind them I saw keen, dark brown eyes—Steve's eyes. She was dressed in a neat cotton-print house dress, and she wore sensible shoes instead of slippers. All this I took in at a glance before Steve said, "Gram, this is Liz Williamson. And this young man is Noah, her nephew."

Noah gave one of his most enchanting smiles and promptly climbed into Mrs. Ames's lap.

She was delighted. "Why, he isn't the slightest bit fearful of me! Is that a storybook you have there, Steve?"

We'd brought along a few books to amuse Noah in case he got bored or needed to be read to sleep. Steve silently handed one to his grandmother, and she began to read Noah a story, using far more animation and expression than I ever bothered with.

It was exceptionally kind of her, I thought, to take time for Noah first, when it was Steve she really wanted to see. But she winked at me as she finished the book.

"It pays to give attention to the small details first, I find,"she said, with a flash of dry humor. "Now, Steve, tell me all about your summer. How were you able to take time away from the farm?" She included me with a glance. "This is such a busy time of year for farmers, isn't it, dear?"

Steve launched into a full description of our farm and the Evans place and told his grandmother exactly what kind of work he was doing. While Noah and I looked out the window, he even gave her the details of his camp in the woods and how he was fixing it up.

She listened attentively. "You really ought to be a writer, Steve. I could see it all, so plainly, while you were speaking." She turned to me. "Well, now," she said, "do tell me how your brother is. I have been praying for him, and I'd like to know his condition, so I may pray more intelligently."

Steve and I, together, brought her up to date on Thomas and the slight improvement he seemed to have made. Then Steve hustled Noah off to the men's room, leaving me alone with his grandmother. I wondered what we'd find to say to one another, but I needn't have worried.

"Elizabeth," she murmured, taking my hand for a moment in her velvety soft one. "I'm delighted to meet you at last, after hearing about you all this time in Steve's letters."

"Oh, call me Liz," I said, trying to hide my irritation at her use of my full name.

But she was a strong-minded old lady, for all her gentle appearance. "If you don't mind, dear, I would like to call you Elizabeth. It was my mother's name, and I've always liked it. Though her name was spelled with an *s*—Elisabeth—as it is spelled in the Bible."

What could I say when she put it like that?

She stirred in her chair by the sunny window. "Steve is a dear boy," she said reflectively. "Really, he's my dearest treasure on this earth."

"He's a credit to you," I said. "He's told me you had a big part in his upbringing."

"Oh, my, not at all." She shook her head, but I could tell she was pleased.

She went on, "I'm glad to know that Steve has found some good friends. His life hasn't been an easy one, you know."

"I guess not," I agreed.

"It wasn't only the divorce, although that was hard enough. But as a Christian, Steve is rather, shall we say, out of place in a public high school. So many times I've wished I had the resources to send him to a Christian school, but the Lord has not allowed that. I'm afraid Steve's lot has been a rather lonely one. The church he attends in Bayport is made up largely of elderly people, I believe."

I hadn't known that. "What about the church he went to with you, in Winthrop?"

Mrs. Ames sighed. "There again, mostly older folks like myself. It's just a little church, way out in the country. There was one younger family when I was there—the Forrests. They were farmers too, with a large produce business. The older girl, Andrea, is just about Steve's age. I had hoped they might become friends, and I think they were, for a time."

"What happened?" I asked quickly. I didn't think this faint prickling sensation was jealousy. Steve hadn't mentioned Andrea Forrest to me, but he hadn't mentioned any of his friends, I realized now.

"Well," his grandmother went on, "I can only speculate, of course. Andie was a very attractive girl: blonde hair in a long braid, dark blue eyes, and a lovely fair complexion. She'd worn glasses since . . . oh, kindergarten. She was the sort of child who looked adorable in them."

I could just imagine. "Andie? They call her Andie for short?"

"Yes, with an *ie*. I don't care for nicknames as a rule, but this one suits the girl."

"I'll bet," I muttered to myself. What was keeping Steve? I wished Mrs. Ames would just tell me what had happened. She was almost as bad as Mom!

"Oh, dear," she said. "I am rambling on, Elizabeth! Why didn't you stop me?"

"I wanted to hear the rest of the story."

"Of course! I'll make it brief. Andie went away to a Christian high school. It seems this school placed more emphasis on charm and poise than on academics or spiritual growth. When she came home for the summer, she was a different girl."

I waited for her to go on. Did this Andie have some claim on Steve? Did they write to each other?

"Well," Mrs. Ames finally said, "I could have dismissed the hairstyle and the contact lenses and make-up—after all, I'm an old woman, out of touch with the times. But her manner had become so bold and flirtatious! She went out of her way to engage Steve in conversation after church, and she even called him on the telephone. I suspect the poor boy was embarrassed by it."

I nodded. "He probably was." I hoped he was.

Mrs. Ames gave me a quick glance. "Well, my dear, I don't want to bore you. What can be keeping Steve and the little fellow, do you suppose?"

I was about to offer to go and look for them, when I heard Noah's unmistakable chatter approaching the door. I poked my head out and asked, "Where have you guys *been?*"

Steve groaned as he propelled Noah ahead of him into the room. "They have a fish tank out in the lobby. I never noticed it on the way in, did you?"

I shook my head. "But old sharp-eyes here must have spotted it."

"I guess so. He made a beeline for it the minute we came out of the men's room. I didn't think I'd ever get him away from it, but when I saw the aides starting around with lunch trays, I figured we'd better get going. I . . . ah . . . mentioned McDonald's, and that seemed to do it."

As if on cue, a plump middle-aged woman bustled in bearing a tray. "Lunch time, Emmy!" she announced, loudly and cheerily.

Emmy! Steve and I exchanged glances. And you didn't have to yell when you spoke to her, either. Her hearing was as good as mine.

When the aide had hurried out again, Steve bent down to kiss his grandmother. "Well, Gram, we really have to go now, but we'll be back again real soon if you think you can put up with us, okay? And you owe me a letter, so I'll be looking for one any day now!"

She smiled, but I could see tears glittering on her pale lashes. "Put up with you, indeed! What kind of talk is that, Stephen Todd? I'll be angry with you both if you don't come again. And bring Noah too. Elizabeth, I've enjoyed meeting you, and spending time with you, more than I can say. I'll be praying for your brother, dear, and your whole family, at this difficult time. Now, Steve, you drive safely, won't you? And come again soon."

She hugged Steve and Noah and shook my hand warmly. I was impressed that she already knew me well enough to understand my dislike of sloppy sentiment.

We didn't talk as we threaded our way back through the maze of doors and corridors. I knew that as soon as we got back to the main entrance, Noah would remember that long flight of steps and would lose no time in reminding Steve of his rash promise.

I wanted to tell Steve how much I liked his grandmother and that the visit had meant a lot to me, but he seemed lost in his own thoughts—who knew what they were?—and I couldn't interrupt. Then we were back in the lobby, where sunlight streamed in through picture windows, and the antiseptic-scented rooms and haunted corridors seemed far away.

As we pushed through the heavy doors, Noah started in: "The steps, the B-I-I-G steps! Up and down the steps!" Steve was true to his word. After the first trip down, I stayed at the bottom, leaning against a stone gatepost and watching Steve gallop cheerfully up and down. He was so patient with Noah—far more so than I was. It was hard to imagine him losing patience with anyone or anything, but I knew that he could, because he had lost it with me, more than once!

Chapter Fifteen

Finally Noah had enough of the stairs. The breeze through our hot car felt wonderful as we headed back down the country road again.

"You know," Steve said suddenly, "we're going to have to drive quite a few miles out of our way to come anywhere near one of those places with the golden arches. I wonder if His Highness would possibly agree to a picnic instead?"

"Picnic!" squealed Noah from his car seat in the back.

"Well," I said, "there's your answer. I think it's a great idea too. I just wish I'd been better prepared, though—I could easily have packed a lunch."

"No problem. I think finding picnic ingredients enroute is lots more fun than bringing them along. We'll just stop at the first likely looking market we come to and get a few things."

When we found a place that looked like a general store, Steve pulled into the parking lot, and we strolled across it. I was enjoying this spur-of-the-moment stuff, and I said as much to Steve.

"Our family picnics were always preplanned. We had picnics a lot—that was the only way we ate when we traveled anywhere—but we usually ended up eating in the car. Even when we went to fast-food places, we ate in the car because of Thomas. I still don't enjoy eating in cars."

"Who could?" Steve said. "It isn't much fun. I guess your parents tried to make it seem like fun, for Thomas's sake. But fast-food places are wheelchair accessible. Thomas could have gone inside, couldn't he?"

"Oh, I suppose so. But it was a hassle, getting him in and out of the van. And he didn't like people staring at him or saying things about him. One time, in the barber shop, a man asked my father if Thomas 'had all his marbles'! Right in front of him! Can you imagine?"

"I sure can. Some people are like that. But this picnic will be different." He opened the door for me and Noah.

He sure ended that conversation on a sympathetic note, I thought irritably, but I was glad he had ended it. Talking about Thomas in the past tense made me uncomfortable.

I managed to push it all to the back of my mind while we wandered around the store picking out our lunch. The deli section was our first stop: Steve chose crusty rolls, bought a pound of roast beef, a container of coleslaw, and a jar of wonderful-looking dill pickles. In the produce section, we settled on a package of gorgeous dark sweet cherries. At the bakery counter, Steve whispered to Noah and then ordered a dozen M & M cookies. Zooming around the store, he swiftly added paper cups and plates, napkins, a package of plastic silverware, a half-gallon of milk, and a little jar of mayonnaise.

Steve insisted on paying for everything, though I was shocked at the total. "This isn't much," he said. "Less than we would've spent at the place we were thinking of. It takes an awful lot of hamburgers, fries, and shakes to fill me up."

Back in the car again, he seemed to know exactly where he was heading. "I've been there only once, years ago," he said, "but it's the perfect spot for our picnic, and I know I can find it again. Just be patient for a few minutes."

We turned off onto a wooded road that seemed to wind along for miles and miles. Steve slowed the car each time we approached a right-hand turn, peering intently into the trees. Finally we turned onto a road that went straight up the mountainside.

"What's up here?" I asked, as we bumped along. Noah looked as if he'd start crying any moment. He was probably tired, and no doubt, extremely hungry. Being good for as long as he had been today must have been a terrible strain on him.

Steve also sensed that something was brewing. "Almost there!"

"What are we doing, anyway—climbing a mountain?" I asked, in a feeble attempt at humor.

"That, Elizabeth, is exactly what we're doing—and here we are," said Steve. "Everybody out! All ashore that's going ashore! Time's a-wasting!"

I looked around me, baffled. All I could see was woods.

"This way," Steve said, shouldering the bag of groceries. He started up a little path that I hadn't noticed, and Noah and I followed.

Noah seemed quite excited by this venture into uncharted country. I was less so, but very hungry, and definitely curious as to where we were going.

Suddenly, the woods seemed to open up in front of us, and we were looking down at the most spectacular view I had ever seen in my life. Down, down we gazed, past hundreds of trees. Below lay a sparkling sapphire pond framed in dark evergreens.

"How beautiful!" I said.

"Pretty water!" shouted Noah a couple of times. But then he began to wiggle impatiently.

"We'll take another look later," said Steve. "But right now, let's eat." He led the way back up the path and into a large open-sided picnic shelter.

Steve plopped the lunch bag down on a picnic table and started taking out the food. "Okay, Liz, you set the table. I'll fix the gourmet feast." He poured milk, made sandwiches, and opened the containers of coleslaw and pickles.

"Ready? Let's pray."

We all bowed our heads while Steve thanked God for the food and asked Him to take care of his grandmother and Thomas. In this quiet place, with the green leaves whispering all around, everything Steve believed somehow made sense. If I could just stay here, maybe I'd begin believing it too. And for the moment, I could even forget that Thomas lay ill, maybe dying, less than a hundred miles from here.

"I could stay here forever," I said.

"It gets pretty cold in the winter, I'm afraid," Steve said, laughing. "But I know what you mean, Liz. It affects me that way too. Have a sandwich?"

I helped myself, along with a mound of coleslaw and a large dill pickle, which I promptly bit into. "Mmm, delicious! I've loved these things since I was a kid."

"Me too. Here, Noah, have a sandwich."

Noah polished off a sandwich, a cup of milk, and most of a pickle. He ate it all without even mentioning "candy cookies"— which Steve had prudently left in the bag.

"Everything tastes great, Steve," I said. "Thanks much for bringing us to this wonderful place. This picnic was one of your better ideas."

"There's more—this isn't all. Have a cookie, then I'll show you the best part."

"Really?" I munched contentedly. "It can't be any prettier than this."

"It is, though."

I was still nibbling on my cookie when he said, "Finished? I'll just run this bag back to the car, then we'll go. Toss these things into that trash can, okay?"

In just a minute, he was back, and we followed him out of the shelter and up a well-worn trail off to the side. We followed its blue-painted arrows; even Noah scrambled sturdily up the ledges on his own. It wasn't the first time today that I was glad his mother couldn't see him. We emerged into an open space.

"The top of the mountain!" I said. "I thought we were on it before!"

"Nope, this is it. And if you liked that view, just take a look at this one." He gestured in a wide circle. There were more ponds, more trees, distant mountains.

I sank down on the warm rock, clasping my hands around my knee. "I love it! How'd you ever discover this place?"

Steve sat down too, pulling Noah into his lap. "We came here when I was nine or ten—me, my parents, and some cousins. We had a picnic too, and we hiked up here. I guess it was about the last time in my childhood that I really felt like a kid. But it was the first time for something too. I'd been to Sunday school by then, and I'd learned a Bible verse. I still remember it: Genesis 1:1. *In the beginning God created the heaven and the earth.* It was the first time I'd ever seen God's creation spread out all around me and recognized it for what it was."

"All those years ago—and you've remembered the mountain all this time?" I asked. "You even remembered how to get here?"

He shrugged. "I told you it was special to me. Later on, when things got tough, just thinking about it was a kind of refuge for me." As he spoke, Steve cradled a sleepy Noah in one arm, stroking the red-gold curls absently. "When Mom and Dad were yelling at each other; when Mom left home and didn't come back for months; when they decided to get a divorce—all the times when things were too hard to take, I could just come here in my mind and be away from it all. I remembered everything: the cool shade of the evergreens, the sparkling water so far below, even the little chipmunks scurrying around for the crumbs we threw to them. It really helped."

"I know what you mean," I said. "While we were eating lunch, I kept thinking that if I could just stay here for a while, I'd get my perspective straight."

He nodded. "It did that for me. Because of the way I connected it with that verse in Genesis, this mountain helped to point me toward God. I began to look through my Bible for other verses with hills and mountains in them. And I found some great ones. Like in Psalm 90, where it says, *Before the mountains were brought forth, or ever thou hadst formed the earth and the world, even from everlasting to everlasting, thou art God.*"

"You memorized it?"

"Yep. And I found the verse that became one of my all-time favorites in Psalm 121. *I will lift up mine eyes unto the hills, from whence cometh my help. My help cometh from the Lord, which made heaven and earth.* I talked it all over with Gram, that first summer in Winthrop. She showed me that there was nothing magical about the mountain itself, but that God had created it and that He cared about me. After I accepted Jesus as my Savior, He helped me in lots of ways to handle my life. The mountain was only one of those ways. But I never forgot it."

Noah was asleep by now, breathing deeply and loudly. I watched his peaceful face for a moment. "I wish I could believe all that as easily as you do."

Steve bent his head closer to Noah's gleaming curls. "And I wish I could understand why you won't."

"I've tried and tried to tell you!" I said. "I want to be *me*—myself!"

He gave me an exasperated look. "Liz, if you put your life in God's hands, you'll be what He wants you to be. And that's the real you!"

"No, it's not!" I brushed a wind-blown strand of hair out of my eyes. "Do you think you're the only one who can quote Bible verses? Here's one for you! *I am crucified with Christ . . .* If I've heard that once, I've heard it a million times. I don't want to *lose* my life! I want to *live* it!"

"But Liz, that verse describes the only way to live. There's a song that sort of paraphrases what the Bible says: 'Let me lose my life and find it, Lord, in thee.' That says it all! If we dare to turn our whole lives over to God, we start to see what He really can do with us."

I shook my head. "I just don't know, Steve. Maybe someday it will make sense to me."

"Don't put it off," he said. "The Bible says, *Now is the accepted time; behold, now is the day of salvation.* If God is speaking to you—and I think He is—better not wait to accept Him."

I moved restlessly on the ledge; my feet were asleep from being cramped so long in the same position. "No," I said. "I can't make up my mind about it so quickly. There's too much involved. Don't push me, Steve."

He stood up, still holding Noah. He seemed to tower over me like the shadow of some Old Testament prophet. "I'm not pushing you. But I'm sure going to keep praying for you. Come on; we'd better get going."

I got drearily to my feet and followed him down the mountain and back to the parking lot. It was one thing to resist the invitations Pastor Nelson gave. It was quite another to resist this one-on-one pleading; I couldn't ridicule someone I admired as much as Steve. It occurred to me that Steve was talking to me exactly as Thomas would, if he could.

We drove most of the way home in silence, with Noah fast asleep. Finally I said very quietly, "Thanks again for taking us up the mountain. It was really an adventure for Noah, and it was an unforgettable experience for me."

Steve smiled, but it was a ghost of his usual grin. "You're welcome. See that you don't forget it. And, Liz, when you think about the mountain, think about the one who created it. If He's got that kind of power, can't you trust Him with your life?"

There was no answer to that, so I didn't attempt one. The rest of the ride was quiet, and I was glad to get home.

Chapter Sixteen

Mom and Dad were eating supper, so we joined them, although I wasn't really hungry, and Steve didn't eat his usual gigantic meal. He'd carried Noah in from the car still sleeping, and the little guy was zonked out on the couch when his parents came in from doing the evening chores.

I saw the corners of my sister's mouth tighten at the sight of Noah's dirty face, still multicolored from cherry juice and several "candy cookies."

"He had a wonderful time!" I said. "Mrs. Ames adored him, and he climbed a mountain and ate a terrific lunch. He behaved perfectly too."

"Toilet training all accounted for," added Steve, saluting smartly.

Mary Rose laughed in spite of herself. "All right, all right! I'm glad it worked out. So you had a good visit with your grandmother, Steve?"

"Oh, it was great. She sure was glad to see us. I won't wait so long to visit her again, though."

Dad spoke up then. "Speaking of visits," he said, "Mother and I are going back to the hospital this evening. We thought maybe you kids might like to come along and tell Thomas about your trip. We told him where you'd gone."

I looked at Roger and Mary Rose. Evening was supposed to be their time to visit.

"We went in this afternoon," Roger explained. "Right now, we're going to take Sleeping Beauty here home and pop him into bed."

"After you wash his face," Steve put in.

Amid general laughter, Mary Rose and Roger left with Noah, and the rest of us headed for the hospital.

Thomas looked just the same. He gazed at us and widened his blue eyes; then he raised his shaggy black eyebrows.

"He's relieved that you got back all right," Mom interpreted.

Yes, the same old Thomas. Still worrying about all of us, even from a hospital bed. I would have given anything if he could be out of that bed and out of this sterile room with its pulsating machines.

I felt awkward, but Steve wasted no time in sitting down by the bed and telling Thomas about Mrs. Ames. "You remember I told you before about her and the home she's in."

Thomas lifted his eyebrows earnestly.

"Well," Steve went on, "she's still trying to witness, even there in that home. She's a lot like you, Thomas. You're lying here silently. People might think you couldn't be a witness. But you are! Nobody comes into this room without seeing Christ in your life and in the lives of your mom and dad."

Unexpectedly, the ICU nurse spoke up. "That's right," she said. "In fact, I'd say that everyone in this hospital knows what these people believe. We can see the power of God in their lives, even if we don't completely understand it."

Steve nodded and went on. "And, Thomas, Gram wants you to know that she's praying for all of you. When she says she'll pray, she means it. She has lots of time on her hands, and she doesn't believe in wasting it. She spends hours praying. She was glad to meet Liz today, and she and Noah got along great."

"Let *me* tell about the mountain!" I put in. "Thomas, we had a picnic at the most incredible place—" and I launched into a vivid description of our afternoon. Steve interrupted from time to time with details of his own, and Mom and Dad asked some interested questions too.

Finally, my parents went off to get coffee. I could tell they thought that maybe this excitement was too much for Thomas. Well, perhaps it was, but I felt closer to Thomas, more like our old relationship, than I had since he'd been in the hospital. I guess Steve must have sensed this too, because he told Thomas that his throat felt dry and that he was going to get a soda.

I sat there quietly for a few minutes. We weren't really alone, of course—a nurse stayed in the room all the time. But, very softly, I began to tell Thomas about the peaceful mountaintop where being a Christian had almost made sense to me. I don't know how long I stayed by that bedside trying to explain myself to Thomas. I only know that, for the first time in weeks, I could be myself with him. Finally we were having that heart-to-heart talk I'd promised myself at the beginning of vacation.

As I talked, I sat with my head bent, fiddling with the pull cord of the window blinds.

A slight movement from the bed, tiny as a whisper, made me look up. Thomas was gazing at me with the most earnest, imploring look in his wide blue eyes. He widened them still farther and looked me straight in the eye.

"I'm sorry, Thomas!" I whispered. "Don't you understand how I feel? Even a little bit? I know now what Steve means when he says he talks with you—you sure are talking to me! I know what you want me to do. But, Thomas, I have to be myself! Can't you see that?"

Thomas turned his head a little bit and closed his eyes. He looked so tired, so weary. A tear edged out of one eye and moved slowly down his thin cheek.

I'm not sure how much longer I sat there, battling tears myself.

Finally Steve rapped softly on the door. He looked into the room, then whispered, "Have a good visit?" When I nodded, he said, "Your folks are with the Nelsons down in the solarium. I told them we'd be leaving soon."

He came closer to the bed, looking down at Thomas. "Looks all worn out, doesn't he? Probably tired of fighting for his life." He touched Thomas gently on the cheek, then straightened up and took my hand. "We'd better go, Liz."

That night in bed, I spent a long time tossing and turning. I just couldn't seem to get comfortable. I'd get to the point where my eyes started to close and I'd snuggle down into my pillows—and suddenly I'd be back in the hospital sitting by Thomas's bed, and he'd be looking at me in that beseeching way. I felt too miserable to cry. I thought and thought—about the whole day, which now seemed about a year long—but mostly about Steve, standing there looking down and saying that Thomas was tired of fighting for life. Something there didn't make sense.

If Thomas really believed all this stuff about being a Christian, then he knew that if he died, he'd be in the presence of God, didn't he? I knew that was what Thomas believed. I'd heard him say so, more than once. So then why was Thomas fighting to stay alive? He wasn't afraid to die. Why, why, was he struggling to live? There must be something—something he wanted to do, or say, or have done for him, that was being neglected.

Something about his funeral? Or his savings account, perhaps? I'd talk to Mom in the morning. Still groping for an answer, I fell into a troubled sleep.

Chapter Seventeen

"Liz! . . . Liz! . . ." I woke up to Mom's insistent whisper. It was still early, probably around six-thirty, I guessed sleepily. The breeze through the open window felt cool and refreshing after my restless night. I stretched, and fluffed up my pillows.

"What is it, Mom?" I asked, through a yawn. "Orders for the day? Guess I overslept."

"Oh, Liz." Mom regarded me sorrowfully. She looked as if she would like to sit down on the bed but, knowing my dislike of chummy talks, she remained standing. Gently she said, "Thomas is gone, dear. The intensive care nurse just called and told us. I thought you'd want to know right away."

"No!" I snatched the pillow from behind me and burrowed down under the covers. Hot tears seeped out from under my tightly closed lids. Thomas simply could not be dead. He was my brother; he was part of me. He could *not* be dead! It was not possible that I would never see him again; never hear his voice calling me Lizard. If I could just stay like this long enough and not be able to see or hear Mom, it wouldn't be true.

Mom waited quietly. She didn't sit down; she didn't even touch me in sympathy. I realized with a kind of dull surprise that she knew me much better than I ever thought she did.

She just waited. Finally I pulled the covers off my head and managed to speak. "Tell me how it happened."

She told me, as carefully and calmly as possible, that his heart had simply given out. "I suppose he was tired of fighting," she said softly. "Thank God, he's far better off now than he has been for years. I don't know, can't even begin to imagine, what our lives will be like without him. But he's perfectly whole and happy now, Liz.

She took a deep breath. "I know how you must be feeling, honey. For a long time, there in the hospital, I didn't want to let Thomas go, either. I prayed that he'd stay alive, and I grasped at every fragile thread of hope as if it were a lifeline. I guess I knew he'd never come back home to us again, but still, all I wanted was for Thomas to just stay alive. Now I see how selfish that was."

"Oh, Mom," I said, "you've never been selfish in your life! You've always sacrificed yourself for one or the other of us kids—even Noah."

She smiled faintly. "It's sweet of you to say so, Liz. But I was selfish to hope that Thomas would live out more weeks, or even months, in the hospital, when there was something far better waiting for him in heaven." She shook her head as if she could clear her mind by doing so. "Now I've really got to get moving. The Nelsons are coming by after breakfast, to help us plan the funeral."

She left the room after touching my shoulder with a feather-light hand. Somehow I got out of bed and went through the motions of getting ready for the day. Even getting dressed was hard. I couldn't seem to look at any of my clothes without thinking of times I'd worn them when Thomas and I had been doing something together. I made my bed mechanically and straightened up everything I could think of. And finally, when I had no further excuse for staying in my room, I went downstairs.

Mom and Dad sat at the dining room table, lingering over coffee. "Mrs. Evans sent us a freshly baked coffee cake, Liz," Mom called.

I cut myself a square of coffee cake and poured a glass of juice, then sat down across from Dad. I was struck again by how much older he looked.

"Are you okay, Dad?" I took a bite of my cake. I knew from experience with Mrs. Evans's baking that it would be very good, but it might as well have been sawdust.

"Sure, honey. I'm fine. Thomas is home with the Lord, and he can rest now. It's just kind of hard on those of us who've been left behind, that's all."

"Thank the Lord we have the Nelsons," Mom added, sipping the last of her coffee. "They'll help us plan the kind of service Thomas would have wanted."

"You mean you never discussed it with him?" I asked.

"He never brought it up," Mom said slowly. "And I couldn't seem to mention it either, especially not after he was hospitalized."

"It would have brought his death too close," I murmured.

"That's right. I don't think he wanted to talk about it. I think he trusted us to make the arrangements the way he'd want them."

I thought that over as I nibbled at my coffee cake. Obviously, over the years, if there'd been some specific way Thomas had wanted his funeral arranged, he'd have said so. No one knew better than I just how outspoken he could be! Mom was right; he would have left it to her and Dad to decide what was best. So it wasn't worry over his funeral that had kept Thomas grasping at life. What, then? I was still thinking about it when the Nelsons drove in.

I wanted to excuse myself, but Pastor Nelson urged me to stay. "In some ways, Liz, you knew Thomas better than any of us. Your input could be very helpful." His gray eyes were kind, and I felt a sudden surge of gratitude to him for not pushing me.

"Okay," I said quickly. "I'll stay."

Point by point, they figured out what Thomas would've wanted. Pallbearers were chosen. Music was selected, including a special number to be sung by our ladies' trio. Mary Rose was in that trio, and I wondered if she would mind; but no one else mentioned it, so I guessed it'd be all right.

There was much discussion over a message. The pastor wanted simply to share Thomas's testimony. "Well, Pastor, " said Dad, "you can work it in, of course, but I know Thomas would want a clear salvation message, with an invitation at the end."

I groaned inwardly, but I knew Dad was right. It was exactly what Thomas would want.

After a little more discussion about other details, the Nelsons went home. Mom and Dad, along with Roger and Mary Rose, would meet with the funeral director after lunch. I was delegated to baby-sit, which was fine with me.

After lunch, Roger and Mary Rose arrived with Noah, and all too soon Noah and I were on our own.

He was grouchy. Mary Rose had said he was overtired; Mom had said he was aware of the tension surrounding him. I wished I could take him for a long, long walk; it would knock him out, and he'd wake up refreshed. But Mom had cautioned me not to leave the house.

"The news is starting to get around now, honey. Folks will be dropping by with food and sympathy. So someone ought to be home. It's important, too, to keep track of who brings what, for writing thank-you notes later."

I'd made no comment. Though I considered the whole idea of bringing food to a bereaved household barbaric, I had to admire Mom's forethought and organization.

What was important now, though, was entertaining Noah. I racked my brain for something new and different. I considered baking cookies, but that would hardly be necessary if we were about to be showered with home-baked goodies.

Play dough! I had a recipe for it in one of my books. I mentioned the idea to Noah; he couldn't wait. We hurried to the kitchen, where we washed our hands and put on aprons; then I dug out the recipe.

"Let's see, Noah, we need flour . . ." He eagerly plunged the measuring cup into the flour canister and poured most of the flour into an old saucepan I set out. "Okay, salt; now, cream of tartar. Hmm, where did that get to?"

There was a knock on the door. I lifted Noah down from the chair, dusted him off as best I could, wiped my hands on my apron, and answered it.

Two women from church waited there, bearing cinnamon rolls and blueberry muffins. "Just a little something for tomorrow's breakfast," one of them said.

I thanked them as graciously as I could and made a note of it for Mom; then Noah and I returned to the kitchen, where I resumed my hunt for the cream of tartar. I remembered using it for a lemon meringue pie but couldn't remember if I'd used it all. Finally I located the small can behind some spices and managed to shake out enough for the recipe. Noah was anxious to stir, and he managed to create a dust storm.

"Okay, Noah, now we measure some water and add some oil and some food coloring. What color do you want?"

He chose green. Wouldn't you know, we didn't have any green; so I measured blue and yellow coloring into the water, and we stirred the whole mess together.

Noah wrinkled his nose. "That not play dough."

"Well, no, not yet. First we have to cook it a little bit."

As I cooked and stirred, the mess got worse. Noah began to hop up and down. "You said make play dough, Aunt Wiz! That tuff not play dough!"

"Just wait, just wait. Maybe it still will be," I said, stirring furiously.

"THAT NOT PLAY DOUGH!" he roared.

"Hey, what's going on here?"

Steve! Between Noah's uproar and the bubbling of the bright green mixture in the pan, I hadn't heard him come in.

"I'm not sure," I said. "It was intended to be play dough, but—"

He scooped Noah up. "Okay, buddy, calm down a second. Let me think. Do you have a . . . uh . . . formula or something, Liz?"

I handed him the recipe. In my hurry, I hadn't bothered to read it all the way through.

"Okay," Steve said. "Hmmm . . . turn out on floured surface and knead until smooth. Got a floured surface handy?"

Quickly I cleared a space on the counter and dumped out some flour. Steve scraped the big green blob out of the pan onto the flour and worked it around a bit.

"Presto! There you are—play dough!" he said. "Want to knead it, Noah?"

"Teve made play dough, Aunt Wiz!" Noah said.

I sank into a chair. "So he did, Noah, so he did." Then I jumped up again, spread a long piece of waxed paper on the dining room table, and equipped it with a child's rolling pin and some plastic cookie cutters. Noah would be all set for hours.

"Thanks, Steve," I said. "You saved the day once again."

"Think nothing of it. How about a cool drink as payment? Got any iced tea?"

"Sure." I filled two tall glasses with ice cubes and splashed tea over them. "Let's take it into the living room."

"Good idea. You look like you need to put your feet up."

I eased myself into Dad's recliner and tipped it back as far as it would go. "Ah . . . that's better. This day seems to have gone on forever, and I've spent most of it on my feet."

Steve plopped onto the couch and stretched his legs out in front of him. "Where is everybody?"

"Funeral home."

"Oh. That's going to be tough," he said. "Picking out a casket and all," he added.

"How do you *know* all this stuff?" I asked.

"Well, when Granddad died, my dad and I helped Gram make the arrangements."

I took another long sip of tea. "Steve," I said, serious now, "tell me something."

"Sure, if I can."

I stared at the green and gold stripes of the braided rug beneath my feet. "How come," I asked, "you always manage to be on hand when I really need you?"

He gave me a direct look out of those dark, piercing eyes. "I think I know, but I'm not sure you want to hear it."

"Oh, I do," I said. The room was very quiet. From the dining room came the muted rumblings of Noah's little rolling pin.

Absently Steve ran a hand along the arm of the couch. "This is going to sound kind of strange," he began. "It might even sound conceited. But it's not meant to be. You . . . you've been to church a lot; you've heard plenty of messages. You know how the Holy Spirit lives in Christians, right?"

"I've heard that, yes."

"And you know that His work is to help us. He's called the Comforter. The Holy Spirit helps us understand the Bible. He's the one who speaks to our hearts and . . . well, helps us to do things God's way."

I nodded, looking into the depths of my glass, swirling the melting ice, not sure I understood his words or liked where they were leading.

He glanced sidelong at me. "So I think, Liz, that it's the Holy Spirit who speaks to me, who puts you into my mind when you need help. It happens."

I had no answer for that.

The silence lengthened. Finally I said, "Well whatever it is, I'm thankful for the way you're always around during the hard times."

He sighed. "Oh, Liz. What if I wasn't around? What if there wasn't a single, solitary person you could turn to for help? Wouldn't it be great to know you had God to help you? He's the one who's really always there when you need Him."

I set my iced tea aside. "When you put it like that, yes. But I just don't know."

"Yoo-hoo! Anybody to home?" inquired a shrill voice.

I jumped. Steve jumped. Noah dropped a cookie cutter with a little clatter.

I hurried to the door, but Great-Aunt Ida was already in. She is a plump, bustling person with bright blue eyes behind gold-rimmed glasses, and a mouthful of improbably white teeth. She is one of our favorite relatives, even though she's one of the most opinionated.

"Aunt Ida!" I exclaimed. "come right in! Mom and Dad aren't home right now, but—"

"I can see your folks ain't to home," she interrupted, fixing me with a stern look. "If they were, it ain't likely you'd be carryin' on with young men. No, I can't stop now. You just take these pies, and I'll come back later. I'm stayin' with cousin Phoebe, so you tell your ma she can plan on me to help with the spread after the funeral."

I winced, but I managed to say, "Wouldn't you like a glass of iced tea, Aunt Ida? You need a break, if you've been baking pies in this heat."

Great-Aunt Ida drew herself up to her full height—all of five feet, two inches—and replied, "Young woman, I can still get more done in a day than you ever thought of. I don't need no youngster tellin' me when I can breathe. But some iced tea would be good."

I fled to the kitchen and clanked ice cubes into a glass. Not a very tall glass, so she could finish it quickly and get back to kneading bread or baling hay or beating rugs or whatever mild activity she had planned for the afternoon. From the living room, I heard Steve calmly introducing himself.

"Well!" Great-Aunt Ida observed as I returned and handed her the glass. "The hired men get younger and handsomer every day! Guess their work's changed some too—baby-sittin' and spendin' all their time in the farmhouse!"

Steve laughed heartily, but I was angry.

"That's not fair, Aunt Ida!" I said. "Steve works just as hard as Dad or Roger or any other farmer. He was Thomas's friend, and he's helped me a lot through this . . . hard time." I'd almost called it what it was: a nightmare.

The old lady drank her iced tea thirstily, walked to the kitchen, and put her glass in the sink. Nothing slack about Ida Simpson! She tousled Noah's curls as she passed him, but he bent more closely over his play dough as if determined not to let her kiss him.

"Who's watchin' out for him during the funeral?" she demanded.

"Mary Rose," I answered, as politely as I could.

"What? She ain't goin' to her own brother's funeral?"

"Of course she is!" I said. "Noah will be going to the funeral with her and Roger."

"Well, I never heard the like of that," Great-Aunt Ida remarked.

Steve smiled at her. "Noah has visited Thomas in the hospital, Mrs. Simpson," he said. "He might not understand that Thomas is really gone if he doesn't go to the funeral."

"Oh!" she said with a sniff. "I must say I hadn't really thought of that." She turned to me. "I'll be goin' now, 'Lizabeth. Phoebe and I are cannin' tomatoes this afternoon. Now, remember to tell your ma she can plan on me—"

"After the funeral," I said quickly. "I'll tell her. 'Bye."

The door had no sooner closed behind Great-Aunt Ida than I turned angrily to Steve. "The 'spread after the funeral,' indeed! That has to be one of the most uncivilized customs in this so-called civilized country! It's like people are celebrating the person's death. It's disgusting!"

"Sit down and calm yourself, Liz,"

When I'd done so—at least, when I'd sat down—he added, "That used to bother me too. But it's really not that bad."

"No? It seems to me like an excuse for a good old family gab-fest. People eat and talk and carry on, as if someone hadn't just died."

"I know what you mean, but, Liz, have you noticed that sometimes it takes a death to remind people how much they care about each other? A family time of talking and eating and laughing together is part of dealing with the whole situation."

"I can't understand how you ever amassed so much wisdom, Professor Todd," I said sarcastically, but I was half serious.

He grinned, then assumed a professorial tone. "Years of experience weathering the storms of life, my dear Miss Williamson. And now," he added, gesturing toward Noah, whose curls were nodding dangerously close to the green blob he was still clutching, "I would advise a nap for young Master Brainerd. In all my days, I have rarely seen a more sleepy child."

Chapter Eighteen

The rest of that day and the two that followed it passed in a painful blur. People came and went with offerings of food, flowers, or just sympathy. I guess I had never realized how many people in Foxville and the surrounding towns knew Mom and Dad. Not only did they know my parents but they also admired and respected them and were trying to help them through this time.

Mechanically I answered the telephone and the door. I passed as many of the visitors as I could to Mom or Dad, who, after all, were the ones they really wanted to see. I arranged flowers, froze food, and made endless lists of who sent what. Roger and Mary Rose did most of the farm work and kept Noah with them. I put together simple meals from the food people brought, and no one complained.

It was like being on a treadmill, and I wondered if these days would ever pass. It reminded me of the feeling you get in a really bad dream, when you want to run and can't move, or when you do run but can't get anywhere.

Steve had told Mom and Dad that he wanted them to feel free to call on him for anything they might need.

Dad, after a moment's reflection, said, "Well, Steve, I'm sure there'll be things coming up that we'll need you to help with. But I was just thinking how much Thomas valued your friendship. I believe he'd like nothing better than to have you say a few words about that at the funeral."

"I'd be glad to," Steve answered, "if you think I could do it. What do you think, Mrs. Williamson?"

Mom nodded, tears clouding her eyes. "I only wish I'd thought of it myself."

Steve hadn't been around much since then. I supposed he was busy preparing his few words. Besides, he might think he was imposing at such a time. But I missed him. He was a link with Thomas—a less painful one, in a sense.

But by Tuesday afternoon, I had stopped thinking about Steve or anyone else. I was sinking deeper into my own personal nightmare, and Dad's matter-of-fact comment about visiting hours at the funeral home just made it worse.

"What?" I asked, unable to believe I'd heard right. "You aren't going to have those—not for Thomas! Are you?"

"Why, Liz," Mom said, "we've discussed this several times, dear. I was sure you knew." She looked helplessly at Dad.

He began to explain. "Liz, the visiting hours are just kind of a chance for folks to say good-by to the way they remember Thomas. Sometimes it's really hard to face the death of a loved one if you don't actually see them in that casket."

I looked around the dining room with its mellow pine furniture and sunbleached curtains. Grandma Williamson's Fiesta dinnerware glowed from the corner cupboard. It was all so familiar, yet I felt like a stranger here. Finally I said flatly, "You don't expect me to go, I hope."

My parents exchanged glances. "We'll leave it up to you," Dad said slowly. "But I hope you'll decide to be there with the rest of the family."

Clearly, there was nothing more to be said.

I went up to my room, but I didn't stay there. I poked aimlessly at my books, glanced into Mary Rose's former room, then drifted across the hall to our old playroom.

This room had once been my favorite place in the whole house. I sank down into a comfortable old rocker and gazed around me at the floppy stuffed animals, the red toy box, the bookshelves crammed full of favorites.

Many days I'd come home from school and gone straight to this room, not even stopping in the kitchen for a snack. It had been a refuge from the hectic, sometimes frightening, schoolday world. Maybe that's why I'd come here now. But the pain of today was a long way from the skinned knees and name-calling of childhood. I rocked idly for a minute.

And what about tonight? I thought over what little I knew about calling hours at funeral homes. I'd only actually gone once, when an elderly relative of Dad's had died. I hadn't liked the unnatural hush of the room, or the disembodied organ music in the background, but the worst part, by far, had been the pale, cold body in the casket, arranged to give the illusion of peaceful sleep.

I tried to connect this memory with Thomas somehow. But it just didn't fit. I knew there was no way I could go through with this, but I had to.

The stairs creaked just then, at the next-to-last step where they always do, and Mary Rose came into view.

"Communing with the past?" she asked. When I nodded, she went on, "I'm looking for a black skirt I used to have. I think it might be in the closet of my old room."

"Going to wear it tonight?"

"If I can find it. I don't have much else that seems appropriate. I've got a dark print dress that'll do for tomorrow, though."

"I'll help you look," I said, but I didn't move. "Mary Rose," I blurted out, "how are you going to get through this?"

She dropped down to sit on the old toy box. "You mean tonight?"

"Oh, I don't know what I mean. The whole thing, I guess," I said. "Explaining it all to Noah, and coping with people tonight—and singing at the funeral. And, worst of all, Thomas—our *brother,* Mary Rose—in a casket. I just don't see how you're going to do it."

Mary Rose regarded me tenderly. "Honey, you're right. In my own strength, there is no way I could do it. But, thank God, I don't have to do it on my own. Moment by moment, as I depend upon Him, the Lord is giving me strength."

I gazed out the window for a minute, at the meandering brook and the old apple trees dreaming in the sun. Then, abruptly, I stood up. "It always comes back to Him, doesn't it?" I asked.

Slowly, Mary Rose nodded. "It does."

I got through the next few hours somehow: eating supper—more accurately, choking it down—showering, getting dressed. Then I was in the van with Mom and Dad; the next moment, we were pulling into the parking lot of Foxville's only funeral home.

We were the first ones there. I followed Mom and Dad's lead in signing the guest book in the hallway. The unusual quiet, combined with the air conditioning, made me feel stifled and breathless. Following Mom, I tiptoed into the room where Thomas was.

My first impression was that the room was full of flowers. They were everywhere. Then, at one end, I saw it: the casket was there, and Thomas was in it. I made myself look, after drawing a deep, steadying breath. And then I let it out in sudden relief. Because that wasn't Thomas in the casket.

Oh, there was a body there, all right. But it wasn't my brother. It was just some funeral director's idea of what Thomas had looked like. As I looked more closely, I saw Thomas's favorite blue sweater, the one he liked to wear to church, and I recognized the tie I'd given him for Christmas. And the thick black eyelashes and shaggy brows were his, all right. It was Thomas, but somehow, he just wasn't there. The real Thomas was gone.

Mom hovered at my elbow. "He looks fine," she murmured, "but he's not really there, is he?"

I nodded. "I was just thinking that."

"He's in a far better place, honey," she said. "See the way we have his Bible fixed?"

Beside the casket was a little table, sort of an easel, with Thomas's Bible on it, opened to the Gospel of John, chapter 14. Verses one through six were underlined.

"That's so everyone here tonight will know the kind of faith Thomas had," Mom said.

Behind us, people were starting to come in. Mom kept her hand on my shoulder and propelled me over to stand beside Dad. Roger and Mary Rose were standing there too, looking solemn and unnatural. Mary Rose squeezed my hand and smiled reassuringly.

The next minute it seemed as if people were pouring into the room. Church friends, neighbors, townspeople, relatives, nurses, doctors, therapists—Mom introduced me to those I didn't know, and I smiled and answered them as best as I could, which wasn't very well. I watched as the others talked and nodded, and as Mom went over to the casket with different people and looked at Thomas with them and gently pointed out the Bible verses. The room was filled with people and the hum of conversation, but for me it all seemed to stand still when Steve Todd walked in.

He came straight over to me, carrying a slim vase containing two yellow rosebuds.

"I wanted to send flowers," he said, "but these were about all I could afford."

And suddenly I was able to say with perfect composure, "Yellow roses were Thomas's favorite. And he'd be pleased that you brought them in person. Maybe we could put them over here?" The mantel of the fake fireplace looked rather empty.

Steve placed the flowers, then looked at me intently. "How are you doing?" he asked.

"Actually, not too well," I said. " I didn't want to come, but I thought I should."

"Could we go closer—to Thomas, I mean?" he asked.

I nodded, and we moved toward the casket. Steve just looked at Thomas for what seemed like a long, long time. When he spoke, it was very softly. "He was the best friend I ever had."

"You'll miss him."

"I will," he answered. "I'm just thankful I could know him for even a little while. And we'll have all eternity together."

Other people approached the casket then, and we went over to my family. Steve left soon afterward.

The rest of the evening seemed unreal, and, in a way, unlike what I'd expected. The muted melodies of old hymns, the serene surroundings, the ready tears were what I'd envisioned. But not the constant buzz of conversation, the reminiscing, the laughter. Laughter, in a room where Thomas lay dead. It seemed so unfeeling. But if, as I'd sensed when I first came in, Thomas wasn't really here, what did it matter?

I pondered these thoughts as I climbed into the van for the drive home. It seemed to take a long time. And the night seemed dark; no moon or stars in sight. It was chilly, the way evenings can be in August in New Hampshire. I shivered. Mom and Dad weren't saying much up front, for which I was thankful, but there was something about this smooth, silent passage through the night that really got to me.

Chapter Nineteen

The less said about that night, the better. I felt chilled, so I put on a warmer nightgown. Then I dozed off, woke up sweating, and opened the window. The breeze refreshed me and I slept again, only to awaken, shivering and groping for my extra blanket. The night was endless, yet far too short. I wanted it to be over, but I didn't want the next day to ever come.

In the morning it was raining—a gray, persistent drizzle that fit my mood. The clock said 9:02; Mom had let me sleep late. I pulled on my woolly old robe, slid my feet into comfortable slippers, and went downstairs.

Mom, Dad, and Steve were seated around the dining room table. I realized suddenly that this was the time Dad usually took his coffee break.

"Have a doughnut, Liz," said Mom. "Mrs. Evans sent Steve over with these."

"Fresh out of the frying pan," Steve said. "Liz, you look exhausted."

"I didn't sleep too well."

Mom poured me a glass of juice. "It wasn't an easy night for any of us, I guess."

Steve stood up. "Well, I've got to get back to work, folks. See you this afternoon."

"Right," said Dad, rising also. "See you then."

After they left, I sat munching a second doughnut and sipping juice. "What's the agenda?"

"Well," Mom said, "after you're dressed, you might get the mail for me and sort through it. That'll be a big help."

I knew what she meant. Ever since Thomas's death, we'd been overwhelmed with mail: sympathy cards from all over, many containing handwritten notes. It all had to be recorded so we could acknowledge the expressions of kindness.

So, after I'd showered and dressed, I tackled the mail. Junk mail got tossed in the wastebasket; business mail and bills were placed in the office for Mom to deal with later. Sympathy cards were opened and set aside for the family to read. As I sorted, I was surprised to find a lavender envelope addressed to me. The return address read, "E. Ames, Ashworth County Nursing Home." For a moment I couldn't think who it was from, but then I remembered—Steve's grandmother! I tore open the envelope with the first real interest I'd felt in anything for days.

It was a sympathy card, just for me. Rather plain and simple, but I was touched that she would take the time and effort to think of me. At the bottom of the card, in her precise old handwriting, she'd written two Scripture references: I Peter 5:7 and Nahum 1:7. I thought I was familiar with the first one—it was something about casting all your care on Jesus. But Nahum 1:7? I wasn't sure I could even find the book of Nahum, let alone have any idea what it contained.

I sorted through the rest of the mail quickly, then went in search of my Bible. For some reason it was important for me to know what Nahum 1:7 said. Finally I located my Bible in a pile of school textbooks. I pulled it out and curled up on my bed, thumbing through the unfamiliar pages until I located Nahum. Chapter 1, verse 7 read, *The Lord is good, a strong hold in the day of trouble; and he knoweth them that trust in him.*

It wasn't exactly what I'd expected, and I considered it thoughtfully. I'd never heard this verse before. *The Lord is good.* Well, I had my doubts about that: hadn't He snatched Thomas away from life—from his family—from me? But I kept reading. *A strong hold in the day of trouble.* Hmmm . . . Mom and Dad had said over and over that God was giving them strength; Mary Rose had told me so only yesterday afternoon. So I guessed that part of the verse was true—for some people, anyway. Then, *and he knoweth them that trust in him.* I pondered that. It must mean that God knew my parents, Mary Rose and Roger, and—let's face it—Thomas. But I didn't trust in Him. And I just didn't see how I ever could.

The Bible was growing heavy in my hands, and I put it on my bedside table. My eyes seemed so heavy—the result of my sleepless night, I knew. Finally I gave in and closed them.

It seemed only minutes later that I heard Mom calling from the bottom of the stairs. "Liz! Lunch is ready! Are you sleeping up there?"

I moistened my dry lips. "Be down in a minute, Mom. I *did* take a nap." I rubbed the sleep out of my eyes and went downstairs to splash cold water over my face.

After lunch, we hurried to dress for the funeral; as immediate family, we were to be there early. In what seemed like no time at all, we were pulling up in front of the white church on the outskirts of Foxville.

I'd never really noticed the beauty of the church before. It was just a place where we went for services. But today I seemed to be aware of details: the soft white walls, the smooth old pine pews with their muted blue cushions, the darker blue drapes at the windows, the mellow woods of the organ and piano at the front of the room. There were floral arrangements of all colors amassed at the front too, and my eye was drawn to the polished oak casket.

Dad had chosen it because Thomas had always loved the huge old oaks that guarded the entrance to our farm lane. And since the casket was closed and all but covered with flowers, it didn't affect me as it had last night.

We filed into the pew reserved for us and sat down. People began to come into the church soon afterwards, and they just kept on coming. I could see the front entrance, so I had some idea of how many people there were, but I knew others were coming in the back door and sitting behind me, as well as in a back room.

When the soft music drew to a close and Pastor Nelson was ready to begin the service, I stole a glance at the front door and realized that even the church steps were crowded with people. Not only were there family friends and church members, but also other people I hardly knew, like the barber who'd cut Thomas's hair, and nurses from the hospital; and people I knew slightly, like my parents' accountant, and teachers who'd had Thomas in school. I looked at all those faces, and I wondered what Thomas would think to see so many people at his funeral.

Suddenly, I knew exactly what he'd think. He'd be glad to see the church so full of people. He'd be so excited that something had brought all these people, some of whom had rarely come to church, together in a place where they could, as he would have put it, "hear the gospel."

Pastor Nelson welcomed everyone, and we stood to sing the first hymn. It was "Channels Only"—Thomas's favorite—and I couldn't help thinking that even right up to the end, Thomas's life had been a channel through which others could see his faith. Somehow, I felt closer now to Thomas than I had for months, closer even than on that last night in the hospital.

Then we were seated again, and Pastor Nelson was reading some of Thomas's favorite verses from the fourteenth chapter of John: *"Let not your heart be troubled: ye believe in God, believe also in me. . . ."*

He continued to read, but he might as well have stopped right there, as far as I was concerned. That first verse burned in my brain.

Let not your heart be troubled. . . and, oh my heart was troubled. It had been troubled for such a long time now. And then, *ye believe in God, believe also in me. . . .* Well, I did believe in God. I'd thought about it a lot, and I knew beyond any doubt that there was a God. His handiwork had always surrounded me in the woods and fields I knew and loved so well. Maybe that was why everything had almost made sense for me that day on the mountain.

"Believe also in me! Believe also in me!" Those words just echoed and re-echoed in my mind. In horror I realized that I was close to tears. There was no mistaking the prickling, burning sensation behind my eyelids, or the painful lump in my throat. "Oh, Lord, I wish I *could* believe! If only I could believe!" I sobbed silently. "But I can't! You'd want too much from me; You'd want to control my life! And I have to be *me!*"

Slowly and emphatically, Pastor Nelson was reading verse 27. *"Peace I leave with you, my peace I give unto you: not as the world giveth, give I unto you. Let not your heart be troubled, neither let it be afraid."*

Peace! I wanted peace so badly. Again I remembered that time on the mountainside when peace had seemed almost possible. I thought of the steadfast evergreens and the calm blue water, and I wanted peace so much that it hurt. Almost, almost, I wanted peace in my heart more than I had ever wanted anything. I closed my lips together tightly to keep a sob from escaping.

As Pastor Nelson introduced Steve Todd as a friend of Thomas's who would say a few words, Mary Rose looked at me questioningly and pushed the packet of funeral-home tissues toward me. I ignored them and fastened my gaze on Steve.

He stood up and moved to the front of the crowded church. As he faced the people, I realized that though he might look calm, he was nervous. He took a deep breath.

"I was with Thomas just a little while before he died," Steve began. "I hadn't known him as long as most of you have, but we'd become close friends this summer. We had that special bond that only Christian friends can have. When I first met him, I hadn't spent an hour with him before I knew how much he loved the Lord. That's quite a testimony, when you think about how some people hide their Christianity from their neighbors for years."

He paused for a few seconds, and there were "Amens" from every corner of the church.

He went on, "But the thing that impressed me most about Thomas was how unselfish he was. He told me once how he felt when he first knew he'd spend the rest of his life in a wheelchair. He was angry and bitter. All he could think about was the things he'd never be able to do. But that was before he knew Christ. Later, when he became a Christian, the bitterness left him, and he began to focus on witnessing to others."

Thomas had never told me that. For just a minute, I felt jealous that my brother would share something with Steve that he hadn't told me. But I forced my attention back to what Steve was saying.

"He really cared about other people, even right up until his death. That last night, when I stood by his bed saying good-bye to him, I felt so bad for Thomas."

Steve stopped for a minute, swallowed hard, and went on: "He was tired, and he was fighting so hard to stay alive. But why? We all know he wasn't afraid to die. So what was he fighting for?"

I'd been wondering about that too. Had Steve come up with an answer?

"I've thought about it a lot," he said. "Why didn't he just let go? And I think that he didn't want to die until he'd tried to reach just one more person for Christ.

"Maybe there are some of you here whom Thomas might've talked to about the Lord. If you aren't a Christian, please think about it today. Thomas would want you to."

He glanced apologetically at Pastor Nelson. "Sorry, I didn't mean to take so much time."

Pastor smiled. "It came from your heart," he said, "and you've just given about half of my message for me."

That caused a ripple of mild laughter and helped to break the tension as the trio got up to do their special song. I watched Mary Rose and thought, How can she do it when her own brother is in that casket, under those flowers? And then I thought back to the afternoon of the visiting hours when she'd said that God gave her strength, moment by moment.

All this went through my mind as the trio began to sing. But I couldn't tell you what song they sang or how it sounded. Because something Steve said had just gotten through to me—something I'd never thought about before—that maybe I was the one person Thomas had been trying to reach before he died.

"Oh," scoffed a voice far back in my mind, "it could have been anybody." And another voice seemed to be repeating the words, *"Ye believe in God; believe also in me."*

I could still hear Steve saying, "He wasn't afraid to die. Why didn't he just let go?" And then Pastor Nelson's voice emphatically stating, *"My peace I give unto you."*

And there in that pew with my family all around, I suddenly stopped fighting. Nothing, no amount of independence, was worth this pain—the pain of having such horrible turmoil inside me, and the agony of knowing for sure that I would never, ever see Thomas again.

I bowed my head—right there, with people on every side—and prayed silently, "Oh, Lord, I do want Your peace. I know I'm a sinner . . . I know just how rotten I've been and how badly I've treated You and everyone else who loved me. Lord, please forgive me for all my sins and make me Your child."

I knew tears were trickling out of my eyes, but I couldn't stop them. I groped for the tissues and finally got the plastic packet open just as Mom pulled a handful out of her purse and thrust them into my hand.

The trio had long since finished singing, and Pastor Nelson seemed to be well into his message. Even though the tears were still pouring forth, I felt a peace such as I'd never imagined flooding over me, sort of like standing in a pool of sunshine on a chilly fall day. Yes, my brother was dead. But I would see him again. The verse Mrs. Ames had put on my card came to mind, and this time it was a comfort to me: *The Lord is good, a strong hold in the day of trouble, and he knoweth them that trust in Him.*

Then it was time to stand up for the closing hymn, "What a Friend We Have in Jesus." Jesus is *my* friend now, I thought. The tears had slowed to a trickle, and I dabbed at my cheek with a tissue. I almost felt like laughing as I realized how much the Lord was already changing me. Just a few minutes before, I'd told myself that I didn't want anyone to see me cry for Thomas. I was too independent! Now I didn't care who saw me, except I did wish they could know why I was crying.

We were among the first people to leave the church, and everyone hurried toward their cars for the trip to the cemetery. As I moved through the door, I felt a light hand on my arm.

"Elizabeth, dear."

I turned to face an elderly lady who had white curls and steady brown eyes behind gold-rimmed spectacles.

"Mrs. Ames!" Steve's grandmother had come to Thomas's funeral.

"Yes, dear. I wanted to give you my condolences in person. Marcia, one of our social workers at the home, was kind enough to drive me over."

Tears prickled at my eyelids at the thought of her caring so much. "Thank you for coming all this way—"

"Liz! Hurry up!" Mary Rose was waving at me frantically, urging me toward the van.

"Oh, they're waiting for me—"

"That's okay," said a young woman who must have been Marcia. "Emmy and I have to get going anyway—we can't go to the cemetery in this rain."

It was now or never. "Mrs. Ames—" I reached for her hand. "I . . . thanks so much for that verse from Nahum, on my card. It . . . it made all the difference. I'd like to come tell you about it sometime, but right now I've really got to—"

"I understand, dear," she said warmly, and as I raced for the van, I wondered how much she did understand. Everything, I hoped.

The trip to the cemetery was quiet, which gave me some time to think. It all seemed so strange. I'd been dreading this final moment more than almost anything else about Thomas's death. And now—though of course I'd miss him, and there'd probably always be some pain in remembering him—I knew for sure that it was just good-bye for a while, because someday I'd see him again.

Strangely enough, as we stood at the grave side with rain drizzling on the canopy overhead, my heart felt light. I could listen to Pastor Nelson's words to all of us, and even though I knew that a gaping hole waited to receive Thomas's body, I could have peace, real peace. I wanted to tell the family about it, but there just hadn't been a chance yet. I did manage to smile tremulously at Mom, but she had no way of understanding what I was trying to say.

Chapter Twenty

When we arrived back at the house, I found myself caught up into getting food ready for the assembled relatives. After all, I'd been cataloging and storing this food for the past few days; I knew where to find it all. As fast as I filled a plate with cookies or sandwiches, Mary Rose or Great-Aunt Ida whisked it away. Mechanically, I heaped bowls with potato chips and arranged homemade pickles in little dishes.

The house was filled with people. I saw Steve on the edge of things, setting up chairs, seating elderly folks, greeting some people. Once I heard a great-uncle boom, "Should've been a preacher!" but I was too rushed to hear any more. The next time I had a chance to look around, Steve was gone. It was like him, I thought, to just be quietly helpful and then tactfully slip away. I wondered if he'd even had a chance to see his grandmother at the funeral.

It was early evening when the last of the relatives finally left. Mom collapsed into an easy chair. Mary Rose and Roger had long since departed for home. Dad was at the barn.

It should have been the perfect time to tell Mom of my decision. But I felt strangely shy. Besides, she had her eyes closed and seemed to be dozing.

Dad came in just then. "Time we were getting ready for prayer meeting, if we're going," he said, heading toward the bathroom.

Mom's eyes snapped open. "Mercy! I'd forgotten it was Wednesday night!" She straightened up. "Well," she said, "none of us needs supper, anyway, after all that food."

I'd forgotten it was Wednesday night too, but I was glad Dad had remembered. This was the first prayer meeting I'd ever looked forward to attending. Always before, I'd been sure that people were praying for me, and it had made me furious. I remembered that old saying 'Today is the first day of the rest of your life,' and thought, For me, right now, that's really true.

Most of the other folks were already at the church when we arrived. It was nearly time for the service to begin. I was glad to see Steve there, sitting with Mr. and Mrs. Evans. I flashed him a smile. He smiled back, then looked at me sharply for a moment. He knows, I thought.

After a couple of hymns and the brief Bible message, Pastor Nelson asked for prayer requests. When people had mentioned a few different needs, he asked, as he always does, if anyone had anything to praise the Lord for.

Dad got to his feet and said how thankful he was for the funeral service and the many people who'd attended, as well as for the strength God had given our family. A couple of other folks mentioned the example Thomas's life had been to them. Pastor Nelson asked, "Anyone else?" and suddenly I found myself standing up.

"I have something to say," I said breathlessly. "I . . . well, I really don't know where to start."

I could see Steve out of the corner of my eye, leaning forward a little. I took a deep breath. "I guess I'll start at the beginning," I said. "I've always been . . . well, pretty independent. Sort of proud. I always thought that was a good way to be. Now I know I was really just plain stubborn."

That got a few laughs. I hurried on. "I didn't want to be a Christian. I thought I'd have to give up too much of myself. And I was afraid to do that. But this summer, through circumstances—

because of Thomas—I've started to see that people do need the Lord. Even me.

"And today—" I took another deep breath and held tightly to the edge of the pew in front of me. "Well, today, during the funeral, I finally quit fighting God. I asked Him to save me."

A few "Amens" sounded softly from around the room, and I could hear people sniffling. But I had to go on.

"When I came home this summer, I'd made up my mind not to go back to Mountainside Christian Academy. But now I know it's where the Lord wants me. And I'd like to thank all of you who have prayed for me for so long, and my family for being so patient. Please keep praying for me. I think—" I paused, and smiled in Steve's direction. "I think there are several good reasons that the Lord wants me at Mountainside."

And Steve smiled back.